And the Stars Were Gold

Annie Campling's first two books, written under the name of Gaye Hiçyilmaz, were *Against the Storm* (Viking) and *The Frozen Waterfall* (Faber). She has based *And the Stars Were Gold* on the experiences of many children in Europe who were taken from their homes in World War II. The bear, Voytek, was a real bear whose story is widely known, and who lived in Edinburgh Zoo for many years after the war.

Annie Campling grew up quietly in England but then spent twenty years in Turkey and Switzerland before returning to a tiny village in Sussex. She lives with a dog, two cats and some of her four grown-up children.

And the Stars Were Gold

ANN CAMPLING

Orion Children's Books
and

Dolphin Paperbacks

With sincere thanks to the Polish Institute and
Sikorski Museum
and to Mr Stanisław Żurakowski and
Mr Wacław Kujawiński who
so generously helped me to tell this story.

First published in Great Britain in 1997
as an Orion hardback
and a Dolphin paperback
by Orion Children's Books
a division of the Orion Publishing Group Ltd
Orion House
5 Upper St Martin's Lane
London WC2H 9EA

A catalogue record for this book
is available from the British Library

Typeset by Deltatype Limited, Birkenhead
Printed in Great Britain by Clays Ltd, St Ives plc

ISBN 1 85881 480 4 (hb)
ISBN 1 85881 481 2 (pb)

Contents

In affectionate memory of Lucian and
for Diana and Ludwick, in whose home
I first heard of Voytek.

1

The House over the Fence

OUR HOUSE ISN'T VERY BIG AND THERE WERE FIVE OF US in it then. I had to share my bedroom with my younger brother Benjy and I'd have loved to move somewhere bigger and to have had a room to myself. Mum always refused. 'This house is more than enough for me,' she'd sigh as she drove the vacuum towards our feet during a day of tense and desperate 'tidying'. By the afternoon she'd be tight-lipped and dishevelled, and we three children, me, Tess and Benjy, would be marooned in a quiet row on the sofa, just in case. I suppose Mum wasn't much of a 'housewife', but we didn't mind at all. Only Mum minded that.

If Dad was home he'd leap up and try to get hold of the vacuum, but she'd hang on grimly.

'Sophie,' he'd protest, 'let me do it, for heaven's sake. Or one of the children.'

'No, don't you bother, Paul. It's too late, now. I've almost finished anyway,' she'd reply in a pained voice, so Dad would shrug and loiter and often get even more in the way. If he was being particularly tactless, he'd remind her about Stef's house at the bottom of the garden – as though she could have forgotten it. It drove her mad. 'I don't want to move,' she'd yell. 'What do I want with *more* rooms?'

Then Dad would say that if we had more rooms, as many rooms as Stef had, then we wouldn't all get on top of each other. And, as he'd said before, we could employ someone to live in and do all the housework. Nowadays, he reminded her, we could easily afford someone to live in. 'I don't *want* anyone to live in!' she'd wail. 'I just want you all to do something. To *help*. I don't want anyone else living here and cluttering up the place even more.'

'I do,' said Benjy, on a memorable Saturday afternoon at the beginning of the summer.

Mum gave him one of her withering looks, but he didn't wither. He grinned and continued to hold his legs out, ramrod straight, so that she had to vacuum underneath them. 'The Edwards always have an au pair living in. They've got Julie this year.' He continued, intercepting her gaze defiantly. 'Julie isn't clutter: she does all the housework for them and she plays cards with Luke and Jim in the evening.'

Jim Edwards was Benjy's best friend and his family lived about four doors away. Mum knelt down to scratch at something stuck in the carpet.

'But I play with you, Benjy,' she said, more softly. 'Look, we'll play something this evening. As soon as I've done supper, we'll play Scrabble. We'll all play, after I've washed up.'

'I don't want to play Scrabble,' said Benjy.

'But you said—'

'I said *cards*,' he snapped, 'not Scrabble. Cards!'

My heart stopped. I thought Mum was going to slap him, and it would have served him right, but she didn't. If Tess or I had been as rude as that, she'd have belted us, but not dear little Benjy. The thing is, Tess and I never were rude like that, we wouldn't have dared. I don't think I wanted to be either, not seriously, and Tess certainly didn't. Tess is kind.

Dad, who had been staring out of the window, swung

round towards the sofa and cleared his throat, but Mum attacked first.

'Don't you dare say anything, Paul! Just don't tell me that we'd be better off in Stef's house, because we wouldn't. I'm not moving into his house, ever. Even if he gives it away. This little house is far too much for me, and you know it, though you won't admit it! It's just too much.'

She switched the vacuum back on and zoomed to and fro in front of us. After she'd passed, Benjy lowered his feet and spat out a small ball of coloured silver paper. It landed silently on the smoothed-out pink carpet and a little thread of spit glistened there for a moment. We pretended not to notice. I felt Tess shiver and we continued to watch the idiotic cartoons in violently-coloured silence.

Sometimes it seemed to me as if Mr Wassilewska's house was like some huge, uninhabited shell on the other side of the fence, waiting patiently for us to occupy it and move in. People said that there had been three houses on that site years ago. Then, one night during a bombing raid in the Second World War, the middle house had suffered a direct hit. The other two had been so badly damaged that all three had been pulled down. The land had lain empty for years. Jim Edwards's grandma, who has lived in this street all her life, remembers playing on the bomb-site as a girl. They had made dens and lit fires and she had had her first kiss from a freckly boy who later became a butcher. It had been an amazing playground where they had dug up all sorts of treasures: spoons, pieces of blue-patterned china, bits of broken toys and rusted things which crumbled away before you could get them free of the soil. Fifty years ago, when the war ended, life had been very different, she said.

Later the land was fenced off and they heard that someone had bought it. Grandma Edwards hadn't taken much notice because by then she was too old to play on bomb-sites. Slowly, over several years, a lone house had been built in the middle of that plot. A foreigner, a Pole with the almost unpronounceable name Mr Wassilewska, had moved in. The trees which he'd planted all around grew swiftly and soon the house was even more isolated. He didn't seem to have a family and often worked away in other parts of the country, so even then the house had an empty and neglected feel about it.

Some people grumbled that it was a waste, when so many families needed homes, but nobody in the street really knew much about their quiet neighbour. The general opinion was that neither he nor his house fitted in very well. Most people couldn't even say his name; they just called him 'Stef' and agreed that he was a bit odd.

His house was odd too. It wasn't just larger than the surrounding ones, it also looked different. The windows were small and outside each hung a pair of wooden shutters with a little heart-shaped hole cut out in the centre. The roof was tiled, but not in the usual red. This roof was tiled in green and was turreted at the corners. High up, under the eaves, there must have been tiny attic rooms. It was almost like a miniature castle. Yet the oddest thing of all was the flight of steps at the back. From a distance they appeared to be carved from white marble, though people said that they were only made of stone. Nevertheless they curved down on either side of the little balcony-like place outside the door and they had iron railings which always looked slightly uneven. Those steps reminded me of really old houses which still have flights of steps down to basements where there used to be flagstoned kitchens and several servants. Mr Wassilewska's house didn't have a basement; it just had these steps, like an afterthought.

In the winter I could see the house quite easily from my bedroom, but in the summer, the trees in his orchard obscured my view. Then I had to go down into our garden to see it. We didn't have an orchard, but we had fruit trees. There were pears along the fences and two apples right at the end. From the very top of the apple tree you could see right into Stef's rooms – or you could do when the shutters were open. Actually, I don't think he used the whole house, because I rarely saw a light on upstairs. People said that he spent all his free time in the kitchen but unfortunately that was on the other side of the house, out of sight.

I used to see him when he sat in the striped deck-chair at the top of those stairs outside the back door. Lately, he seemed to spend a lot of time out there doing nothing at all, but just sitting, with his tanned face tilted back towards the sun. He was a tall, thin man, with white hair and faded dark eyes. Sometimes, he'd be there in winter, if it was bright enough. I've seen him sitting out for an hour under a pile of blankets or coats, when there's been snow on the ground. He reminded me of our tortoise who could be tempted out of hibernation by a couple of sunny days. We always had to make sure that he didn't topple over on to his back when he tried to climb out of his cardboard prison. He'd have died if that had happened.

I suppose Stef must have known when I was up in the apple tree in winter, but he never waved or gave any sign and neither did I. In summer it was different. I spent hours perched up there looking at things. The taller tree was quite difficult to climb. About three feet up from the ground the trunk divided into two. One part was sturdy but short, the other had raced away above everything else in the garden. Dad was always threatening to prune it, because he said we couldn't reach the fruit, but I always managed to pick them. I climbed with an old laundry bag slung round my neck and lowered each apple carefully into that. I hardly dropped any. At the top, if you're balanced properly, you can stick your head out beyond the leaves and then right over the roofs to Telegraph Hill. On a warm summer day, you can feel the air move and see things that you would never have seen otherwise. I've seen a little fluffy nest of spiders hatch out up there and I saw the men who broke into the Edwardses actually making their getaway over the back fence. I didn't realise they were burglars: I thought it was a gardener or window cleaners or someone like that.

Our other apple is only good for children's play. Its trunk is thick and knobbled where the lower branches have been cut off. I used to put swings on it and last summer I built a tree house in it for Tess and Benjy. It was really nice, with a rope-ladder which they could draw up after them. But if you want to live dangerously and see things, then you must climb to the top of my tree.

I'm sure I could have seen plenty of things from Stef's house too, especially from the attic windows, but none of us had ever been in, though Dad had always wanted to, and Stef had invited him often enough. And Dad wasn't the only person who was curious. It seemed that half the people who passed by thought that this odd house at the back of our garden was somehow their 'dream house'. People were endlessly wanting to buy it. Complete strangers knocked on our door or called over the hedge. Did we know the name of the owner of the large white house behind ours? Was it on the market? Did we think that the owner was likely to be selling in the near future? Because if so – it was *exactly* the house that they had been searching for . . .

Dad always replied to these inquiries very coolly. He said it was a cheek and that they were probably all property developers who wanted to tear the house down and put up flats instead. Mum was more sympathetic. She said that property developers didn't have old estate cars full of grannies and pushchairs and fat labradors. She always told these people that yes, she thought the house was for sale because the owner had offered it to her. She agreed that it would make a lovely family home. She would even print Stef's name for them on the backs of petrol receipts that they found on the floors of their cars: MR STEFAN WASSILEWSKA. And she'd wish them luck.

That made Dad wild, because if any family deserved to have that house, it was us. It was perfect – apart from the steps. And that was the first thing he'd do: he'd take the steps away, he said.

'Why?' I asked.

'Because they don't fit in. They're pretentious,' he explained.

When I asked Tess what that meant she said that pretentious people showed off and Dad said, 'Exactly.' That was the problem with that house: it looked as though it had been designed to show off, to look down on other people's houses. 'But I thought you liked it,' I had said, puzzled.

'Oh I do. But it needs sensible landscaping. It needs to be made to fit in with everything else. Then it wouldn't seem so out of place. It's the steps that are the real problem. Without those useless steps, it would be ideal.'

He never talked like that when Mum was around because it would have infuriated her. Years ago, when I was about two or three and Tess was still a baby, Stefan Wassilewska had actually offered the house to my parents. Dad said that he was practically giving it away. The story became part of our family history. Apparently, one hot summer night, just after we had moved into our house, Mum had been walking up and down the back garden trying to get baby Tess off to sleep, without much success. Tess, who is so quiet and sensible now, had been one of those demon babies who screamed all the time. Dad always says that it was a double shock for poor old Mum because I had been such a good baby. So there was

Mum, walking up and down with this baby yelling its heart out, when suddenly, somebody spoke to her over the fence.

'Madam,' Mr Wassilewska had said, in his strong Polish accent, and he'd touched his hat, or lifted it, or whatever foreigners do. She'd turned around, startled and offended, and there he'd been in the dusk, looking over the fence at her with his panama hat in his hand. He had stared intently.

'Madam, please, dear madam, would you not, with this baby, be happier to come and live in my house?' he had said. Or something like it, for I think his exact words have changed over the years.

'No!' Mum had cried. 'No thank you!' She could have fainted with fear and dropped Tess, she said, but she'd managed to keep calm and say something very English and cutting in reply and then she'd come running in to Dad in floods of tears, because 'that dreadful man' had said something really insulting!

Dad had gone round straight away to sort it out and had come back saying that it had all been a misunderstanding: Stefan Wassilewska really was a perfect gentleman. He had only been trying to offer to sell his house to Mum because he thought that she and her young family would have settled in there more happily. Mum always shook her head when this story was retold. According to her, there had never been a misunderstanding over the garden fence. It was Dad who hadn't understood, and never would.

I was supposed to have been sound asleep upstairs in my little blue bed during this incident. I'm sure I was, but I'm also sure that I can remember Mum running upstairs. I used to be terrified of the dark and people had teased me and said that real boys shouldn't be scared, so Dad had painted this special bed for me. It was dark blue and the head and the foot were decorated with mountains and a silver moon and then these beautiful golden stars. When the bedroom curtains were open at night the light from the street lamp fell on these stars and they shone, just a little bit. They didn't stop me being afraid, but they made me feel much better, and I can remember Mum rushing into the room and tearing me from my warm nest of dreams in that blue bed. Her beautiful face was splashed with tears and moonlight and somewhere in the background Tess was still screaming inconsolably.

Despite this unfortunate beginning, Mr Wassilewska continued to offer to sell his house to my father. Apparently he had other houses and didn't need this one. But it was no good. Mum just wasn't interested. If we met him in the street he'd smile and raise his hat and say something to us, but he never seemed to notice Mum, which was curious, because everybody else did. She said that he was 'creepy'. Why hadn't he got his own family, if he was so keen on filling up that house? she wanted to know. Dad said that she should show more understanding; that he was a charming elderly man who had ended up living in a foreign country after the war.

'Then why doesn't he go back?' Mum would ask cruelly, which wasn't like her. She didn't mean to be cruel. She'd have given the coat off her back to help someone in trouble – and had once. It had been in London at the première evening of one of her films and I'd been so embarrassed because she'd only had this minute red evening dress on underneath. The press had taken photos of her trying to give her coat to this young beggar, but the beggar had backed away and the coat had fallen between them on to the wet pavement. The captions under the photos had been awful but I know Mum had meant it kindly. And that's why I didn't understand why she seemed to be so unpleasant about Mr Wassilewska.

She absolutely forbade us to go into his garden, and

Dad went along with the ban. It was considered 'dangerous territory' like the railway lines or those fenced-off bits at the bottom of telegraph poles, with their yellow 'danger of death' triangles, warning you to keep out. I didn't break her rules, and nor did Tess, not even for 'official business', like collecting for charity or delivering misdirected mail.

Dad said that good mothers couldn't help worrying and that it was part of our job, as nice children, not to add to Mum's problems. He said that he expected me, as the eldest, to be totally trustworthy, and I was. So Tess and I never went into the garden over the fence.

Only Benjy did that. I'd watch him from high up in the apple tree. He'd amble down to the bottom of our garden, glance around, then push aside a loosened board and slip through the fence as stealthily as a rat in the night. In winter, I'd see him tread a defiant line of footprints into the snow-white lawn and break up the ice at the edge of Mr Wassilewska's pond. In autumn, I've seen him kick apart the piles of rustling, golden leaves and in early summer the rough scent of blackcurrant would drift up to me in the rising warmth. Then I knew he would be hurriedly pushing the leaves aside and tearing the clusters of berries from the bushes with greedy purple hands. I didn't really spy. I usually turned away and looked in the opposite direction towards Telegraph Hill. There, pin men and women walked their dogs and gangs of children rode the hillocky bits on mountain bikes.

I really wouldn't have minded if Stef had crept out of his house and down the curved white steps and made his stealthy way past the tall reeds and the pond and through the laden, leafy orchard to where that little thief was gorging himself on stolen fruit. He could have seized Benjy by the back of his T-shirt and grabbed his blond curly hair and dragged him, screaming and kicking, to the far side of the house. He could have imprisoned my little brother in a rabbit hutch and fattened him up on poisonously sweet Polish cakes and I wouldn't have minded one little bit.

2

Scratching out Stars

IT WASN'T BENJY WHO DISAPPEARED AND AFTER IT HAD happened I'd have given anything not to have had such treacherous thoughts. But it was too late, then.

In the winter of 1995–6 Mum did a pantomime. It wasn't a local thing but a proper London show and it went really well. She had to share a dressing room but this time the other actor was helpful and understanding, Mum said. They even swapped herbal remedies for migraine. The show finished in February as planned and when spring came Mum bought loads of stuff from the garden centre and worked like a slave planting it all out. Both she and the garden looked great. People pointed her out as they passed by in the street, but in a nice sort of way, and she did a few autographs over the garden gate with her hands all muddy and twigs in her hair. By three thirty in the afternoon she was always tidied up, with fresh lipstick and her hair brushed out, and then she went down the road to the school like any other mother, to meet Benjy. That spring, I wouldn't have minded being seven again: then she could have met me and then everybody would have wanted to be my best friend.

Instead, now that I was thirteen and in secondary school, Mum and Dad were keen for me to be 'independent'. That meant that I had to freeze for hours at bus-stops and then be terrorised off the best upstairs seats by these enormous fifth-form girls who kept telling each other in shrieking whispers what they'd done with their boyfriends the evening before. They made it perfectly clear that somebody like me wasn't boyfriend material. I acted the cold fish and tried to look down my nose at them, but really, I was pretty intimidated.

Lucky old Tess was safely out of it. To everyone's surprise, quiet Tess had won a scholarship to a boarding school and had gone there the autumn before. She seemed very happy but I missed her a lot. She's one of those thin dark girls with very neat straight hair, cut in a dead straight fringe. I'm dark too but nobody would ever call me neat and tidy, though they could call me 'dashing', if they liked. Tess's school work is immaculate too. People can never decide if she looks like Mum or not, but everybody agrees that their characters are totally different: Tess would never offer her coat, she'd already be on the side of the beggars. Yes, I really missed her, and I wonder now if Mum had missed her too.

Anyway, spring and Easter were fine and then, in June, Mum's agent telephoned. He left the message with me, and when I told Mum, her whole face lit up, and she clapped her hands. 'What did he say, Richard? The exact words? Can you remember, darling?' she purred.

'I wrote it down for you. He said: "Tell your mother that the job's hers, but I need to know tonight."'

She called back straight away and said yes. Then she had terrible doubts. Dad reassured her. 'Of course you're not being typecast. You did pantomime in the winter and now this. You're not old either so you can't look old. You said yourself that other people have turned the part down because it's too challenging. Don't tell me you're afraid of a challenge, Sophie?'

She didn't answer and they talked about other things, principally about the lovely money that she would earn.

Dad rummaged about in the freezer and found some forgotten pizza and we had that with champagne to celebrate. We talked excitedly about every single thing of importance except that this film was to be shot in Los Angeles. Neither of them mentioned it, and nor did I, though I knew. The agent's message hadn't been quite what I'd written down.

'Oh Ricky darling, how's things? Look, can you tell that mother of yours that if she still insists on that LA job, then I think I can swing it. But I've got to know tonight. Twist her arm, there's a good boy, Ricky. Get her to make up her mind, eh?'

Well, anybody who still doesn't know that I hate being called Ricky deserves to have their message jumbled up, don't they?

So nobody mentioned Los Angeles all weekend, which was stupid, but we didn't want to spoil things. Tess, who is a weekly boarder, was home too, but on Sunday evening, just as Dad was about to drive her back to school, she tried to ask Mum about America and Los Angeles.

'What time will it be over there?' she said anxiously. 'We've got these special times at school for phoning, and with the time difference . . .'

'Goodness, darling, how clever of you to remember! I suppose there must be a difference but I don't know whether it's forward or back, but you mustn't worry. You can phone any time!'

'But we're not allowed to, Mum!'

'But you would be if it was important.'

'If it was important, yes, but . . . but . . .'

'What is it, Tess? Is there something you haven't told me about? Goodness, Paul, stop the engine, so that Tess can tell me.'

'It's nothing like that.'

'There must be something. I don't *have* to go. I mean I

haven't actually signed anything so I can . . . decline, can't I? I can say, "sorry, my daughter needs me" – I won't go, Tess, if you've got a problem.'

'I haven't,' said Tess.

'I have,' said Benjy.

'Goodness, look at the time,' cried Mum. 'You'd better put your foot down, Paul, you know that they don't like them to be late back on Sunday evening. 'Bye, my angel!' She kissed Tess, then hurried towards the house. Tess and I waved until the distance and the evening separated us.

Benjy had raced up the drive after Mum. He ran at her with such force that she stumbled and might have fallen if she hadn't grabbed the doorpost.

'Steady on, Benjy. I haven't even gone yet!'

'I won't let you!' he screamed.

'Oh, don't be silly. Anyway, you'll be fine. Auntie Beatrice is coming to look after you.'

'I hate Auntie Beatrice!' he muttered, with his face buried in her stomach.

'You don't,' I said, because he didn't.

'I do. I hate her. And I'll hate her even more. I'll hate her so much she won't stay and you'll have to come back. I'll sick up all the food she cooks . . .'

'That'll be fun,' I said.

We both looked at Mum. She reached behind her and tried to pull his hands apart, then she must have stuck her nails in, because he yelped and jerked away, but she grabbed him and lifted him up against her, although he was really much too big for that.

'You won't really hate poor Auntie B will you?' she whispered, rubbing her cheek against his, so that they were both wet with tears.

'I will,' he said. 'I will. I will. I will.'

Then she nipped his little pink ear with her white teeth and he mewed and thrashed like a kitten who didn't want to be petted, but she clung on. Eventually she struggled up the stairs with him and crouched beside him on the little blue bed which used to be mine, and she stroked his hair while he cried himself to sleep.

Later, when she'd gone to her own room, I heard him turn over and stretch and mumble through clenched teeth: 'I will. I will.'

At the last moment, when the taxi was already in the drive, Mum panicked. She sat at the foot of the stairs and kicked her suitcase away with the toe of a new pair of red shoes.

'I shouldn't be going,' she said.

'Of course you should,' I said. 'We'll be fine, honestly.'

'Won't you miss me?' she asked.

'Of course we'll miss you,' said Tess sensibly. She had got special permission to come home for a day to say goodbye. 'But we still want you to go. Don't we?'

Dad and I nodded. Outside the taxi honked again.

'And you'll all look after Benjy?'

'Sure. Don't worry, Mum.'

'And watch that he doesn't wander off?'

'Yes.'

'And water those new shrubs, especially that rose . . .'

'Come *on*,' said Tess and picked up the smaller case encouragingly.

It was strange. I didn't feel at all miserable about her going. In fact, I felt quite excited about it, as though *we* were doing something different. Well, we were in a way: Dad had been shopping and filled every spare shelf and cupboard with food. And not just everyday food either. He'd bought things like maple syrup and chocolate-flavoured breakfast cereal, special things that we don't usually eat. Then we'd changed the house around to put a bed in the dining room for Auntie B, who was coming on Sunday evening, and even that seemed fun. To be honest, I was pleased that she was going away and the only sour note was struck by Benjy who refused to come down to say goodbye.

If it hadn't been such an important day, Dad would have yanked him out of the cupboard where he was hiding, and somehow shaken or bribed or shamed a 'goodbye' out of him. But that day we just left him – we were all being so careful not to spoil things. We daren't risk an unpleasant scene. So only Tess and I kissed Mum. Tess cried. Dad enfolded Mum in his arms and we saw him push aside her hair and kiss the back of her neck and then hug her again and the taxi driver joked about it and said 'Couldn't I have a kiss?' and she said 'Yes,' and kissed him lightly on the cheek and then she settled herself elegantly into the back of the car and looked suddenly at ease. Tess and I waved and waved but she didn't look back. Dad just sort of stood there with his head on one side and scuffed at some weeds on the drive and Benjy never got to say goodbye. Ever.

She didn't phone that evening, and Dad said it was probably jet lag. He called, but the hotel couldn't get a reply from her room. He said that the receptionist at the hotel sounded particularly stupid. He laughed it off, but he stayed by the phone all night, waiting. Tess refused to go back to boarding school and Dad didn't want to take her in case he missed the call from Mum. I didn't want them to go: I didn't want to be left alone in the house because suddenly, I dreaded having to answer the phone. Each time it rang we all stopped breathing for a fraction of a second before a voice that wasn't hers broke our hearts again.

On Sunday it was in the papers. 'Actress and Mother of Three, Sophie Styron, Disappears.'

I can't talk about it. I can't begin to tell you what it felt like. Other people seemed to know more than we did: she'd checked in at Heathrow, she'd got on the plane, she'd taken a cab to the hotel and gone up into the room that had been booked – or at least a woman looking like her had done all those things. The girl on reception at the hotel hadn't noticed anything strange – hadn't noticed anything, to be honest, and hadn't known who Sophie Styron was. She'd just checked a Sophie Styron into the hotel, as booked, and thought no more about it. And why should she? Actresses are two a penny in LA. And there was even the headline in one paper: 'Who Was Sophie Styron?' and they printed all sorts of dreadful lies about 'the secret lives of this popular actress' and Dad tore it out of my hands. He ripped it up before I could read it through, but I had had time to see one thing: 'It is understood that Sophie Styron has been reported missing on previous occasions.'

I didn't ask Dad about it, but I felt that it was true. I couldn't exactly remember anything, but I recognised the panic and the horror from some other time. It even comforted me, in a strange way. If she'd come back once, she could come back again, couldn't she?

I was glad that Auntie Beatrice was still coming to stay, although I didn't exactly know who she was. She was one of Dad's friends and not Mum's, but Mum had always liked her very much. She was older than them, and I think Dad may have worked for her at one time. In a way she was as much their auntie as ours. We all liked her, even Benjy did, whatever he pretended. She had often come to stay and she'd helped Mum when Benjy was born. She and I got on really well because she made a fuss of me, like I was still a little kid, and that's quite nice now and again. She'd brought sugar mice for everyone on her last visit, and I'd eaten mine nibble by nibble, nose first, but I think soft-hearted Tess has still got hers.

So if anyone could help us, it would be Auntie B and I was desperate for her to arrive. I spent that Sunday at the top of the apple tree, listening for the sound of her little old Citroën. It was quite nice up there, watching and waiting: some of the smaller apple leaves still had their white spring down on them and the fruit was barely formed. It tasted of nothing much but stalk and sourness and I couldn't swallow it but had to spit the stuff out.

I could see Stef in his deck-chair at the top of his steps, and I wondered if he'd heard about Mum. And if he had, did he care? There were people out on Telegraph Hill, joggers by the speed of some of them, and I couldn't believe that they were up there, unconcernedly enjoying themselves. I leant back against the tree-trunk, and I thought, if I just lean back further I'll fall. I'll fall down through the branches in a shower of smashing twigs and floating leaves and I'll probably break something, like a leg, and then Mum'll hear about it and have to come back.

Or maybe wouldn't. In which case I'd know, for sure, what she was really like, and then I'd tell everyone, so that all those people out on Telegraph Hill, who were carrying on with their lives as though nothing had happened – all those people would know, and feel sorry.

Then, about four o'clock, I heard Auntie B's car. I let myself down the tree far too quickly and scraped myself quite nastily and needed a plaster, but I had to get to her before Benjy did. If he got there first and started being hateful straight away, he'd spoil everything, because she was our last hope. He and I ran down the drive neck and neck but I managed to trip him and he went flying. It must have hurt because he had blood on his lip and his knee, but he got straight up before I could offer a hand and he actually said 'Sorry Richard,' and sniffed hard to stop his eyes from watering. I was just dumbstruck. He grinned at Auntie B and grabbed hold of her case and began to stagger back towards the house with it.

'She's *here*!' he yelled, as though we hadn't noticed. 'She's come!'

Auntie B and I gathered up the other odds and ends

and followed him in silence. Dad and Tess were waiting at the front door.

'Come *on*,' Benjy was yelling from the dining room. 'We've put your bed in *here*, oh, hurry up, Auntie B, I've done the flowers for you, I got them specially.'

'Have you heard anything?' She looked at Dad.

'Not really,' said Dad, and I thought he was going to cry, but he didn't. He turned to Tess.

'How about that tea, old lady?'

She nodded and went.

'Why don't you help?' Auntie B suggested pointedly, so I followed Tess ungraciously, dismissed like a naughty child. We fiddled about at opposite ends of the kitchen, not looking at each other.

'She's disappeared for ever, hasn't she?' said Benjy, suddenly bursting in.

'No!' we both shouted simultaneously.

'She has,' retorted Benjy.

'She hasn't,' Tess's voice trembled.

'Then where is she?'

'People think she may have stage fright, that she's just lost her nerve for a bit,' I said, making it up as I went along. 'Actors do that . . . all the time.'

'They don't! And anyway, she's still disappeared,' said Benjy. 'I knew she was going to. I tried to stop her . . .'

'She *hasn't* disappeared!' I roared. 'She just hasn't phoned. That's different!'

'Oh yes?' He looked at me with pity, as though I were the younger brother and he the elder.

'I don't think that she'll ever come back,' he said, 'and that's why I'm going to use her special headache pillow. She said I could, if I couldn't sleep.'

Then Tess dissolved into tears and I hated Benjy more than I'd ever hated him before.

During the following weeks neighbours gave us cakes. The kitchen was overflowing with cake and we even had it for breakfast, as though somehow cake made a difference.

'We just thought you might enjoy a bit of home-made sponge,' those kind ladies would say, as they appeared at the front door. They didn't want to come in, later maybe, but definitely not now. In fact they were so keen to get away that they wouldn't wait to get their plates back and we've still got several plates that aren't really ours. At school, teachers asked me about Dad and about 'poor little Benjy' 'who was too young to understand'. Some people asked after Tess and said that it must be especially hard for a girl to lose her mother. Other people never said anything at all. Mrs Edwards was one of those.

She and Jim turned up as usual on Friday evening to take Benjy to the cubs just as though nothing had happened. And Benjy trotted off without a backward glance at us.

I don't know which was worse. Maybe nobody can say 'the right thing', but they could try, couldn't they? One of the few who did was Mr Wassilewska. When I answered the door he took off his panama hat and looked down at his old-fashioned, polished shoes.

'Please,' he said, 'please accept my sadness for your great loss. I am very, very sorry for you, and your brother and sister and your father. And for your dear mother.' Then he made a little bow.

I wondered if he'd written it down before he came, to be sure that he'd get it right. Then he sighed, and shook his head and kept turning his hat round and round in his hands as though he didn't understand it either. 'She was so beautiful, your mother, like –' but he couldn't finish his sentence and I'd already turned away. Auntie B came out and said something to him while I escaped to my room.

When I looked in the sitting room later, they were playing Scrabble. Benjy was snuggled against Auntie B.

'I don't want to make *that*!' he whimpered, 'even if it gets me more points. I want to make TIN!'

I left them to it and went back to my room. Benjy had decamped. Now he would only sleep in Dad's bed with his head on the scented silk of Mum's special pillow. He'd even moved his little collection of china animals on to her bedside table. The little blue bed was empty and abandoned. I climbed carefully into it and curled up. It creaked uncertainly under my weight. Over the years when he had used it, Benjy had scratched out the moon and there were only a few bits of star left, and these didn't shine. I hugged my knees up to my chin and didn't dare stretch out in case the bed fell apart under me.

Much, much later I woke. Surely the phone had rung? I started up, but one of my feet was trapped under the bars at the end of the bed. When I'd got it free I couldn't hear the phone any longer, but I knew it had been ringing, even if no one else in the house had heard it.

And I would have got to it, if my foot hadn't been trapped.

3

The Best Pears Are Eaten by Bears

I DON'T REMEMBER WHAT WE DID IN THE REST OF JUNE
and July, except that Auntie B stayed on and we three
continued at school. I don't think anything much did
happen until August the 8th, which was Benjy's birthday.
His always has been an extraordinary birthday date: the
8th, of the 8th, 1988, and this year was extra special
because it was his eighth birthday. He couldn't stop
talking about it.

'It is special, isn't it?' he asked, and we'd nod, and agree
yet again. He was arranging the little china monkeys that
Tess had given him in a neat circle.

'I'll never have another birthday like this, will I?' he
persisted. 'Will I? Dad? Will I? When I'm old, Auntie B,
when I'm 28 or 88, or 188, will it be special like this? It *is*
special, isn't it?'

He was really boring about it. Tess hadn't been stupid
like that on her eighth birthday. I'd given her water-
colours and a matching sketchbook and she had settled
straight down and painted me a little picture of a fox to
say thank-you. I gave Benjy money, a ten-pound note in a
birthday card, which said 'Hello 8-year-old.' It was what
he'd asked for, after all, but he hardly thanked me. He
wanted to know if I'd told the people in the card shop
about his special birthday date and when I shook my head

he looked really disappointed. He got lots of cards and had ripped them open without bothering to look where they were from. He didn't mention Mum. He never even got up early to look and see if there was a foreign-looking envelope or stamp. I did. I always got up early now. I had to reach the post first, just in case.

I don't think he was at all disappointed that she hadn't sent a card. He was much more interested in his birthday treat. Auntie B was taking him and Jim Edwards and another friend for a day out to a theme park. I suppose Tess must have gone too but I can't actually remember that. I just said that I didn't want to go. I absolutely refused. Dad got upset, he said that I couldn't be all alone in the house, but I still wouldn't go. In the end Auntie B agreed that maybe there wasn't enough room in her little car, so I might as well stay. Dad shrugged and left for work, and said he'd phone me at lunchtime, to check.

When they'd all gone I walked through the hectic rooms that were now suddenly still. I pushed open the doors and smelt where people had slept a few hours before. In their bathroom her round white Jasmine soap lay untouched in its green glass dish. She'd banned us from using it. Now, I fished out the litter of ducks and boats and flannels that Benjy had left behind. Then I ran a stream of clear, hot water into the bath. I undressed and stepped in and it almost scalded my ankles and feet and made me hop from foot to foot. But I let it run. Then I stroked the jasmine-scented bubbles all over my skin and I ran the water so deep that I could nearly float.

I glimpsed Mr Wassilewska from the bathroom window as I was drying myself. He was walking round his orchard looking up at each tree. That was when I thought of the pears. I had been wanting to speak to him for ages, but I couldn't work out how to manage it. I'd thought of throwing a ball over the fence and then asking if I could get it back, but that seemed awfully childish. Then I thought of just slipping through the paling, like Benjy, only I ruled that out because I might get stuck or he might catch me at it.

Now there were the pears. We'd had a bumper crop and Auntie B had suggested that we should give some away. I could truthfully say it was her idea, if anyone asked, and it gave me a serious reason for going into his garden.

I wanted to ask him about Mum. I didn't know what the question would be, but I knew that whatever it was, it had to be asked carefully, face to face, and not breathlessly, over the fence. And there was no one else to ask. Everyone, the police, friends, family, people she'd worked with, they'd all drawn a blank. The people who knew her didn't know what had happened to her, so maybe this stranger who didn't know her, might have some ideas.

I arranged some of the best pears in a wooden bowl and went round to Mr Wassilewska's front gate. My heart actually thumped so much that I couldn't undo the latch straight away. It struck me then that I'd lived in our house for ten whole years and had never once been through this gate. Of course, that was true of lots of other houses, but you're convinced that you know somewhere really well and when you think about it you discover that you're actually a stranger in your own streets. I looked up at the house and for the first time I wanted to know something about the man who lived there. I didn't want to be a stranger any longer.

'Well,' he said, as he opened the door, 'how kind of you and your aunt. How very kind.' He picked out one pear and held it in the palm of his hand and smiled. 'And how could you know that this is my favourite fruit?'

'I didn't. I mean, they're just pears and we've got too many . . .' It sounded so rude and ungracious and I can't think why I said it, but he didn't notice.

'And I, too few.' He laughed. 'I am always so jealous of

your tree, which is good, I think, every year. Whereas mine is no good. Flowers? Yes. Fruit? No! And then there is the wasp, the great British wasp. You have the wasp too?'

'Yes, a few.'

'Ha!' His voice was loud. 'You know what they say about pears?'

'No.'

'The best pears are eaten by bears!' He laughed vigorously at what must have been a joke, though I hadn't understood it.

'Please, I do not make a joke about your family.' He looked anxious when I didn't laugh.

'No. No, I know . . .' But I didn't.

'I will explain to you the joke,' and he'd taken me by the arm.

He led me round the side of the house to the steps at the back, where his deck-chair stood out in the morning sun. He rummaged through an untidy pile of blankets and boots and umbrellas inside the back door and brought out another chair. He opened it up. 'Oh my,' he said and energetically dusted out what must have been several years' accumulation of spider's webs and dead moths and dried leaves. I wondered if anyone had ever sat in the chair, because deep inside the unfaded colour was as brilliantly orange as if it were brand new.

'Not so many visitors,' he laughed. 'Just earwigs and woodlice on Sundays.' He flicked a couple off.

'Mr Wassilewska,' I said, 'was Mum . . . a visitor . . . ever?'

I hadn't meant to ask it straight out.

'Yes. She did visit me. And—'

'Never mind.' Suddenly I didn't want to hear more. 'You were going to explain that joke!' I interrupted.

'Of course. Right. Now – you know what bears like best?'

'Honey?'

'Yes. Well done. But why?'

'Because it's sweet?'

'Top of the class again. Now – where are the sweetest pears?'

I tried to think, but couldn't. Had she sat here too? And seen this view?

'Where is the sunniest part of the tree?' he prompted.

'At the top?'

'So?'

'The sweetest pears are at the top. But . . .'

'Think!'

'Oh wow! I get it. Only bears can climb to the top of the tree and get the best pears.'

'Correct. It is what you say when you are a bit jealous and someone, maybe your neighbour, has something better than you and you say, in secret to yourself, of course – "Ha – he may have a finer carpet than me, but he's only a bear."'

'I see. That's really good. Were you a teacher, Mr Wassilewska?'

'No. Not I. But my father was. A high-school teacher, "gymnasium" we called it in Poland. And he always talked like that to us, like a teacher. I do the same thing maybe?'

He leant back and looked away into the distance and suddenly I understood why the house had been built this way, with the steps here. From here, at the top of the steps, you could almost see for ever. The view swept up the valley, way beyond Telegraph Hill and beyond the suburbs of the town, to where the wheat fields lay over the backs of distant hills like golden fur. In the lost, blue distance, the shimmering might have been mountains or might have been the sea itself. It was amazing.

'Did she sit here?'

'Yes.'

'And saw this?'

'Yes.'

'When?'

'A long time ago. I think you were a baby, or a very little boy.'

'So have I been here before, Mr Wassilewska? Did she bring me?'

'No,' he said, but he hesitated.

'So where was I? Where did she leave me?' Had she danced off before, visiting neighbours, and leaving me all alone in my little blue bed? Had she left me all alone and frightened in the night?

'You were just over there, in your garden. You were not far away.'

I didn't understand. If she'd come, why wasn't I allowed to? Maybe she'd been right and he was odd and creepy and I shouldn't be here at all. She must have had a good reason for disliking him and his house so much, mustn't she? Had something happened here, between them?

I got up, but I didn't really want to go. He got up too. I could think of nothing more to say. No, that's not true. I had so much to say, but couldn't begin. Then I remembered the neighbours' cake plates.

'Please,' I lied, 'my aunt asked if we could have the bowl back.'

'Why, of course. How thoughtless of me. Come.'

He went inside and I followed and with that one step was in another world. It was not like a home at all, for it was almost empty. The walls and floors were lined with wood, smooth golden planks that here and there were marked with knots and whorls. There were framed photographs on the walls and a chest at one side, but that was all. The great body of the house was unoccupied and unfurnished: more museum than home.

'A moment, please.' He paused before a door and went through and shut the door behind him.

I didn't follow. I heard him opening cupboards looking for something. Near me, in a gilt frame, there was one photograph of a large family group outside a house: of parents maybe, and children, and dogs lying on the ground. The children were leaning over an iron railing at the top of a flight of steps. There was a little girl in a pinafore and ankle boots and a young man in army uniform. It could have been this house, but it wasn't, not quite. But it was his face. It was his thin face with his downward-sloping brows that made him look sad. And that, surely, was him, seated in a carved wooden chair, with a baby in a dress on his knees and a dog at his feet.

'No,' he said, when I asked. 'That's not me. That's my father.'

'The teacher?'

'Yes. And that's my mother, and that – how do you say it, my nurse, my nanny – she helped my mother –'

He pointed them all out. Brothers, sisters, the cousin in army uniform, his father's brother, his grandmother.

He handed the empty pear bowl back to me.

'That's me,' he pointed to a small boy in the foreground, 'I think.'

'Don't you know?'

'Yes, I think I know. But I can't remember.'

'Can't somebody tell you?'

For a moment he remained silent.

'There's nobody left to tell me,' he said at last.

I looked at the photo. That, too, had been a sunny day, for the shadows were hard. The children were scowling towards the sun. One even shielded her eyes. And those, surely, were summer dresses, and the baby's little feet were bare. It must have been summer then too.

'There is just me,' he said, 'just that boy, there.'

I didn't know what to say, but I suppose he did.

'You think your aunt could spare some more pears –
for this old bear?'

'Yes, of course. Shall I go back and get them now?'

Then I remembered that Dad was going to phone.

'Actually, can I bring them this afternoon? After I've
picked some more?'

'Why not? And I will make you coffee instead of tea.
We will have coffee at your teatime. Yes?'

When Dad phoned I didn't say anything about visiting
Stefan Wassilewska, though I told him I'd picked more
pears, and he was pleased. He might be late, he thought. I
nearly said 'Again?' but didn't, because I knew that he
sometimes met up with people who'd known Mum, just
in case. Anyway, it would give me more time. I picked the
pears and some apples as well, and ate cereal and crisps
for lunch and then, as it was only one thirty, I went into
the sitting room to turn on the television but instead I
took down our family photo. It was taken years ago when
I was about nine or ten, and Benjy was a toddler in a
sunhat. I'm dark-haired now but I was fairer then, and
plumper, and Benjy was all soft pink tummy with fair fluff
sticking out from under his hat. Tess looked just the
same: neat, cool, tidy and clean, even though it had been
terrifically hot on that holiday in Italy. My parents had
rented this house on a mountainside, with a donkey in the
field at the back. I don't really remember what Mum and
Dad did all day, but Tess and I had played in the field
with that donkey.from morning till night. And there it was
in the photo in its straw hat. Dad had bought one just like
it and worn it. And every evening all five of us had walked
hand in hand down that steep little track into the village.
We ate ice-creams at a café and then walked back with
Benjy asleep over Dad's shoulder. At night when Tess
and I were supposed to be asleep we'd hear the two of
them laughing and giggling on the veranda outside. We'd

hear the rustle of leaves as they picked grapes from the overhanging vines.

That was the first time I'd eaten fresh figs and slices of water melon. It had been perfect and none of us had wanted to lock the door behind us and come home.

In the photo Mum was wearing a blue checked shirt and cut-off jeans and was so tanned. I blotted her out with my thumb and then I slowly spread out my fingers so that the rest of the family disappeared.

The phone rang after I'd left the house. I hesitated with the bowl of fruit in my hands. Then it rang again, I turned, but didn't really hurry, and when I listened at the door it wasn't ringing any longer, and I wondered if I'd imagined it.

Mr Wassilewska was waiting for me.

'And where is my fruit thief today?'

'Benjy?' I was rather shocked.

'Of course.'

'It's his birthday.' I explained about the birthday trip and I said I was sorry about his blackcurrants.

'And my flowers!'

'Oh no!' I had wondered where the flowers he'd picked for Auntie B had come from.

'Oh yes! And last year, some goldfish, I think.'

'I didn't know . . . honestly. Well, I didn't know about the goldfish.'

Then I saw that he was smiling at me.

'My little brother was like that too. Always so naughty, and they don't punish him, not like they do me. Because I'm older, I must be sensible, always sensible. "You are the headmaster's son," they'd say. And what was he? The headmaster's puppy dog? But of course I never said that to my parents.'

'There,' he said, pointing to a chubby little boy, 'that's him.' We were looking at the old photo again and I saw that the date on it was 1936. 'He was a real thief.'

'You mean . . . really?'

'Yes, I mean that. He really stole.'

'Didn't he get caught?'

'Yes. The secret police arrested him twice, I think, but he got free, maybe they felt sorry because he was so young. Mind you, I stole too, but he was always better than me. I was a coward.'

Then he stopped and looked at me. 'You know what happened in the war, don't you? In the Second World War. They've told you what happened in Poland?'

'Not really. Maybe a bit.'

'Shall I tell you?'

'All right.'

'It's a long story.'

'Auntie B and the others won't be back till quite late.'

'Then there's no problem.' He laughed, a loud barking laugh, and rocked back in the deck-chair. And I was surprised at the energy of such a quiet man, whose white hair was always neatly combed.

'How old are you now?'

'Thirteen.'

'So. I was just a little older. I was fourteen at the start of the war and like you, not so tall, not so short, and everybody was bossing me around. That night at the start of the war I was asleep in bed, in a feather bed, under a new winter quilt that my grandmother had made for me. It's not like your duvets here; it is a thick woollen quilt that goes into a white embroidered cover and I can remember it today. It was so warm in bed. And suddenly there's this noise, this dreadful noise in the house and dogs are barking – not our dogs, but another sort of bark altogether and I was so scared. It was 1940, just at the end of the first winter of the war and already we have heard things: people are being taken away in the middle of the night. Suddenly my mother came in, still in her night-dress, with a jacket on top, and I realise that it isn't morning. It is the middle of the night. Downstairs I hear men's voices and they are speaking Russian, shouting it, I should say. I recognise Russian a little because since the Russians entered our country in 1939 we weren't allowed to study Polish in school, only Russian. So my mother says 'Get up, get up' and I can't. I'm stupid like you are in the middle of the night. Then this soldier pushes past her into the room and I can smell him: he stinks! He smells so bad and his face is filthy and his hands are dark with dirt. He puts his filthy hand out to grab me and then he sees the quilt and I think he's shouting "Get up" too, but not so unkindly. He's looking at the quilt, which is not silk – but shiny like silk – and I hear his rough hand, as rough as wood bark, catch on the threads of that cloth as he strokes it. His jaw drops – like an animal he is – and he half smiles. You know the story in the Bible? – don't cast your pearls before swine. He is like that swine, that ignorant pig. Then my little brother wakes – he stumbles in blinking, still half asleep. Then he sees this ugly man with his coarse red face, this stranger in our house, and you know what he does? He runs at him and he beats him on his legs and my mother screams and the man picks him up, hauls him up by one arm and my little brother is yelling and I'm terrified that the solder will kill him – will smash his head against my bedroom wall. They did that sometimes. You know about the Russian army do you? . . . They killed people like you might kill rats. And you know what I did that night?'

I shook my head.

'Nothing,' he said bitterly. 'Nothing. I just sat and shivered under my red quilt.'

'I think,' I said, 'I think you were just afraid, Mr Wassilewska. Very afraid. I would have been.'

He nodded, biting his lips together. Then he went into the house to make the coffee, and I remained outside and rested my cheek on the iron railings.

4

The Silence of a Crowd

*I*T WAS BEAUTIFUL COFFEE, WITH WHIPPED CREAM
floating on top, which he said was the Polish way, but
the cake was even better. A friend's wife still made it, he
said, with lots of poppy seeds and walnuts, and I was
lucky because these were the last two slices.

We both felt better after we'd eaten and he dusted the
crumbs off in a determined way and put the tray on the
ground.

'I didn't make sense, did I?' he asked.

'You did, only . . .'

'Exactly. Only I should start at the beginning. The
trouble is, I don't know where that is.' He paused and
though he looked down the valley, I don't think he saw
what I saw.

'Could you start with your family?' I suggested.

'Yes. Yes, I could.' He nodded at me. 'With my father.
You're right. That's a good place.'

'He's the headmaster of the gymnasium?'

'Yes! So I did make some sense? Good. And my
mother. She was a teacher too, but now she only looked
after us. We were six children, four sons and two
daughters. We weren't poor, but we weren't rich. There
were rich families in town and a few very rich ones, some
merchants and landowners and the Nadels who owned

the glass factory. They were very rich. We were a comfortable family, with plenty of nice things to eat and the forests just outside, well, half an hour's walk away. And that was all I cared about, then. My mother had relatives all around the district, my grandma was still on her farm with my mother's brothers. So we had plenty, honey, eggs, mushrooms, walnuts, fruit, wool; and that red quilt.' He laughed. 'That wool was from my grandmother's sheep. She had washed the wool and cleaned it herself; she had been to the market in town and chosen the red cloth, and sewed it for me, with her own hands. She worked hard, people worked hard, and it was not easy but we got by. Winter especially was not easy. In the old house we did not have water indoors, but in the new house which my father built, he put in a kitchen with a sink and tap and a bathroom. Not a bathroom like here in England but a tiled room with hot water in a big copper, where you lit the fire underneath. And there was plenty of wood, with enough for everyone, in the forests. Have you seen forests in winter?'

'Not really, just on the television.'

'Well, that gives you an idea. They are so beautiful, I'm telling you, so very beautiful and bright with frost and snow that is blue under the moonlight. One day, when you go on a sleigh, at night, you will understand their beauty. Of course, in winter we had fun too, we all skated and skied. Everyone did, boys and girls.

'In that first winter of the war we still skated, it was what I liked best. I was more interested in speed-skating than in girls. I was a little fool. We all are: we can't help it. So we raced, my brothers and my friends and my cousins. We raced on the lake, until the thaw came, and the thaw is bad news. Everywhere is mud then, but afterwards in spring, you can go to the forest again. I was a boy scout. My friends too. We spent our life outside in the woods.

We picked berries, nuts, fungi – you know, like mush-rooms – very good to eat, but you must be careful. My father knew which were poisonous – I always took them back to him. We made fires – we played. I don't know what we did . . . but we were very happy.'

'I know what you mean, Mr Wassilewska. We went to Italy, to the mountains, for a holiday, and we stayed outside all day! And just – played. Me and Tess.'

What had we really done, I wondered, apart from lying spread-eagled on that steeply sloping field and look up at the sky through shut red eyelids? I'd done that for hours on end, and never felt bored.

'You know Italy?' he asked.

'A little.'

'You've heard of Cassino? The Battle of Monte Cassino?'

'I'm afraid not.'

'Don't worry. You will when I've finished with you!'

'That house,' I said, remembering the photo of the family group on the steps, 'is that house with the steps the house your father built?'

'No. That was our old house, in town. Let me see: I was about nine or ten in that photo, in 1936. There is no picture of the new house, except in my head.

I think my father had the land for the new house for some time and when he had saved enough money, he started to build. I went with him up into the forests, with Michael, who was the forester. We walked up through the trees after the thaw, and my father and Michael chose them, one by one. That man, Michael, he knew trees. He said to my father "Take this one and not that." And then the men cut them down and hitched them to the horses and dragged them clear of the forest. And I still remember the smell of the fresh-cut pine – I loved that new house so much: I watched it being built for, maybe, three years, day by day and month by month.

In those days some people employed special crafts-men to saw the trees into planks. My father did that. He liked these people, though others said they were just gypsies. My father said, no, they were fine craftsmen. He was a kind man, my father, though very strict. Not, how you say it here, a joker? Not a joker, but a gentle man. So, he asked these people to build for him. They were from Russia, very unusual people, with great, uncut beards and old-fashioned ways and those strong hands like horses' hoofs, and they moved around all the time with their families. They cut our wood. They sawed wood better than your sliced bread. I've never seen anything like it. They put the trunks up on two trestles and then they started: just two men on either end of the saw, with their arms sawing to and fro, and the sawdust falling like a fountain. It was magic.

And it was so nice when the house was finished and we moved in. For me, it was like a palace carved out of amber. All the inside was golden and it smelt of pine. Too much, my mother said, but I liked it. I loved it. Before, in the old house, we had been right in town and it was fine, but there was not much room and always there was a task for me to do. "Stefan, get me some more water. Stefan, take these boots to the cobbler. Stefan, go and see if there is fresh fish today!" But in the new house, I was free. I escaped out of the back door in the early morning and only came back as night fell.

We spent the first winter of the war there, in the new house that Father had built, though he was not there; he was already in the army, of course, and that was sad. Especially at Christmas, I remember. But during those winter evenings my mother continued to make all those things that Polish women make – cushions and rugs and curtains and those pictures, tapestries. And they were all very bright and colourful with flowers and birds. That's why I had a new quilt, of course, for my new room. We all did. I was thirteen, I think, when we moved in.

I was in secondary school, not yet in the gymnasium, though my second brother Jan was there. My oldest brother, Edward, he was in military school. Then there was me, Stefan, the third brother. And there was Josef – my little brother; Josef the thief whom we already speak of, and lastly, Maria, who was very little indeed, not yet at school when we moved into that house. Let me see – ah! I forget my sister Stanislawa, she was my elder sister. She was already married, much too young, mother said, married against everybody's advice, but Stanislawa didn't listen. Who listens, anyway, when they are nineteen and in love? But she didn't go far after marriage, only to the next village, where her husband's family had a farm.

And that is why, when the Russians came in the night, on Saturday 13th April, 1940, they didn't find us all at home. My father was in the army, already arrested by the Russians, we knew that much. My mother had a letter and he had asked her for rubber boots, because of the thaw. You can have mud up to your armpits in the thaw and I remember my poor mother trying to find and then send him those rubber boots. He was in a prison camp, with many others.'

'Did he get the boots?'

'No! He was already dead when she got the letter. He didn't need his boots. But we didn't know it.

By that time Edward was in the army too. Again, we don't know where, and that very night my mother had sent my next brother, Jan, to see if my newly married sister Stanislawa is all right, because her young husband is also in the army. Jan takes Maria with him, because already there is not so much food in town and my mother plans that maybe we join Stanislawa in the country, where we can hide and wait, because there are Russian soldiers all over our town. Everybody is saying that Nazi Germany cannot continue fighting in the West and the East at the same time and that the war will end soon. If we can only wait quietly somewhere, we will be all right. Of course, they're wrong, but we believed them. We wanted to believe them.' He sighed and shook his head.

'So that night, when the Russian soldiers came, there was just you and your mother, and your little brother, Josef, in that new house?'

'Yes.'

'But *why* did they come? What did they want?'

'They came to take us out of our country, Poland, and into their country, Russia. They took us prisoner, so that they could have what was ours.'

'What, everybody?'

'No. Not everybody, but many – a million. You look in history books, you can read this. Many more than a million, nearly two million were taken away!'

'Who did they take?'

'People who were a little bit important, shall we say. Doctors, priests, mayors – my uncle was a mayor, they took him, with his wife who was an invalid; such men they take first; the people who had organised our scouts and guides, they took them; teachers, like my father. Later we learn that they prepared these lists of the people they will transport months before and then, when they were ready, they came like wolves in the night and dragged us out.'

'But why?'

'So that no one is left to say "no" to them, when they steal our country. They hope that those left will run around like headless chickens and not know what to do. They wanted what we had – our lands, our houses, our factories, our forests, and our people!'

'But you can't just take things!'

'Oh yes you can. They took me and my mother and Josef, just like that.'

I almost wished that I hadn't come. I didn't want to hear about anything else going wrong, yet I suddenly had to know what had happened, in the end.

'What did the soldier with the dirty hands do to Josef? The one who was holding him up by his arm?'

'He shook my brother off like a mouse that has run up his sleeve, and Josef fell down, plop, on to my bed. But he was not hurt. That man was, I think, just a stupid brute, a pig, and was only interested in what he could steal. Now I know that these people had nothing in their own houses, nothing. They could not believe what they saw in ours. So while this brute is stuffing into his pockets whatever he can get, another soldier comes upstairs. Maybe he was an officer because he read to Mother from an official paper: we, the Wassilewska family, were enemies of the Soviets, and so we were to be deported – sent away – as "special deportees". We had half an hour to pack, he said, and we'd better hurry, because the train wouldn't wait!

And all the time their dogs were outside, barking, and their muddy boots were stamping all over the newly waxed boards of the house and I could smell their sweat and their anger. I was so frightened I couldn't dress myself. My mother had to come over and do up the buttons on my shirt. Then she started shouting at me and at Josef to hurry and I was putting things into a bag and she was pulling them out and saying "don't be stupid, you don't need that," and the soldier was shouting at all of us, saying "Hurry, hurry." And I can't believe it's happening and I nearly go out in bare feet into the night, but Josef finds my socks and boots for me, squats down and ties up the laces. I manage just one sensible thing: I pick up my boy scout rucksack, and put it over my shoulders as I leave my room.

My mother has hurriedly packed whatever she can in a laundry basket, and she slips on the mud outside the house and some of the clothes fall out and, in the confusion, Josef runs back into the house. He's looking for our dog and I think the soldiers will shoot him, but they don't, they chase after and as they do so my mother says to me that there is a secret sack of clothes already packed in the woodshed and that I must go and get it. "How?" I cry, because the rest are standing around us with fixed bayonets. "Do you want me to risk being killed for a bag of clothes?" I weep. "Yes," she says, very coldly. "Tell that soldier what you are going to do, then do it." And I do. In schoolboy Russian I tell him, as politely as I can, that I have another bag in the woodshed. And he looks up from his list of names and says "Yes. But be quick," as though this is an everyday occurrence. I feel my way in the dark and touch the sack and for a second I think – if I hide here, maybe they'll pass on and forget me. But I don't, of course. I pick up the sack and put it over my shoulder and go out into the moonlight, where they are all waiting for me.'

'And that's how you left that house?'

I remembered how she had left without looking back.

'Yes. And do you know what was so bad? It was walking along that road to the railway station in town. It was *my* road. It was my road where I met my friends, every morning as I walked to school, here one, there one, this one late as always – he was a greedy boy who liked his breakfast too much, and on the right, past the church, my best friend, who was the dentist's son. And now I walked along it quite alone. Oh yes, my poor mother was there, stumbling with the laundry basket, and a bag, and my little brother was there, still crying loudly that we must go back for our dog. And the soldiers were there crying "Hurry, hurry" with those terrible dogs, straining on their leads.

I saw lights on in one or two houses, even at that hour, but nobody came out to help me. Not a window was opened. No curious face looked out. And I kept thinking, somebody will run out and save me. They'll shout: "Hey, it's a mistake, that's Mr Wassilewska's son, he's a good person, you've got the wrong boy!" '

'But nobody did?'

'Of course not. I told you I was a fool. As if *anyone* deserved to be arrested! And of course some of the people from those houses were already at the station: my best friend with his father, the dentist, and his mother. They were there and so was our German teacher.'

'And then?'

'They make us line up and wait and wait. Finally they make us climb into railway carriages. Not carriages like you have here; those were like the wagons that you put post-office sacks and bicycles in, only without windows. We three climbed in together and my mother was very pleased because families who have their fathers with them lose them then. Suddenly some of the men are separated from the women and children and taken away. Then everybody is screaming again. My best friend's father was torn away from them like that, and my friend cried.

So, they pack us into the wagons and there are bunks, like shelves made of wood: so they have been planning this, we understand. It is getting dark and we can't see where anything is, but we manage to get on a bunk, the three of us together, and other people are treading on us and climbing over us to get to the bunks above, but we hold on to our place and push some people away.

Then they shut the door and for a second, I'm pleased. Perhaps it will be warmer now. Then we hear the bolts fastened on the outside and when we hear this we are as quiet as if we had all died. Then, people are jumping up and banging on the doors and screaming. And do you know what I do in this chaos?'

'No.'

'I sleep. I can't think how I do it. I stretch out and yawn

and my mother puts something soft under my head and I sleep and sleep.' He's smiling as though at a pleasant memory.

'I slept all the way to Italy in the car. I missed everything,' I said and immediately thought how stupid and insensitive I must have sounded, but he didn't seem to think so.

'One must sleep,' he agreed. 'My mother knew that. She was a clever woman, she let me sleep.

When I wake up it is still night, but the train has stopped and I think "Where are we?" and I'm happy because we can't have gone far, if it's not morning yet. Now others are asleep and I am awake, so I creep to the side of the carriage and I peer through one of the slits and what do I see? Our station. And then, a voice I know whispers right into my ear, "We haven't gone anywhere yet, you idiot!" and it's Peter – not my very best friend, but another good friend from school, and I'm so pleased. It's as if I'm lucky all of a sudden. I have found this friend and I never think to be sad for him because he's a prisoner too. He tells me that the train has been in the station over twenty-four hours and all that time more people are being brought. And for the first time I'm furious. And you know why? That they didn't give me time to pack! I didn't think that this should never have happened – I just think, like a fool – "Oh, if we had had twenty-four hours, I could have brought my stamp collection and chess set and – and something to drink." For, as soon as I think about home I imagine our stove with a kettle full of hot water for coffee, and then I was desperately thirsty. And when you think of drinking, then you want to pee, yes? Oh, I can tell you, I was sad I had woken up.

And you know where we have to do it? In a hole on the floor of the wagon. And then I understand what the bad smell is! Maybe we were forty people locked in there together.

Then, as dawn comes I see that we are not quite alone. Outside the station, people have been gathering quietly. More and more people are arriving and though we cannot hear their voices, now and then we hear the clip-clop of horses' hoofs, as more carts move towards us. Still more come. They are trying to get to the train but the guards hold them back. They carry bundles of food, I suppose, and clothes, and they want to give them to us, but they cannot. Each time someone approaches the train they are beaten back by the guards, but they do not go away. We are watching them through the cracks in the wagon walls, and they are standing beyond the track, watching us. Now the crowd won't be quiet. Daylight paints a cruel scene. Then my mother cries out. "Whatever is it, Mrs Wassilewska?" people ask. She cannot speak but she points.

It was my brother Jan and my two sisters. I recognise my little sister Maria – because she is in my brother's arms. She wears this hat of white rabbit fur that she liked very much. I begin to shout to them: "Stanislawa! Maria!" But my mother claps her hand firmly over my mouth, so I'm dumb.

"Hush," she says fiercely, "do you want them to be taken prisoner too? Stay quiet, so that they can go free!"

Then the people around her protest, "Don't talk like that, we *aren't* prisoners, Mrs Wassilewska; they will just take us to another district, out of the way of the fighting. We will be home soon."'

'Was that true?' I asked him.

'No! My mother fell silent but didn't move from the side of the wagon where she could see her other children. Then a hush descends: something is happening, that is clear. We all hold our breath and wait. Have you ever heard the silence of a crowd?'

I shook my head. 'The soldiers are moving swiftly up and down outside the wagons checking the bolts. Then the wagons jolt and this great sound rises up above the slow grinding of the wheels, the clanging of the pistons and the sudden hiss of steam. People were singing. I was singing and my mother too. Together with all our people who had not let us go alone, we sang our national anthem as the train began to move.'

He got up and took the tray into the kitchen but I stayed there and cried for the first time since she'd left.

5

Distant Territories

'YOU SHOULD HAVE HEARD HER SCREAM,' REMARKED Benjy cheerfully. We were eating supper at home after they had all returned from the birthday trip. Auntie B blushed.

'It's true,' she confessed. 'I'm hopeless at things like that. I really was scared.'

'I wasn't,' said Benjy, 'specially not today!'

'Well,' she began serving out the ice-cream, 'if you want me to come for your birthday next year, you'll have to choose a different treat. I couldn't do that again.'

I waited for Benjy to say that she wouldn't be needed next year, because Mum would be back, but he didn't. He just grinned and licked the chocolate ice-cream from his spoon in a way that Mum had always disapproved of. I shivered in the silence as if a chill draught had slithered into the house and frozen our hearts. It happened all the time now: whatever we did and wherever we went, something always reminded us that Mum wasn't there. You couldn't open a paper or watch television without somebody mentioning, at worst, a disappearance, or at best, a 'one-parent family'. It always made me catch my breath.

Only Benjy didn't notice: I don't think he missed Mum at all. Now he giggled.

'Honestly, Auntie B,' he explained, 'they're only *rides*. And you can't fall out. Ever. I wasn't even a tiny bit frightened.'

'You were,' protested Tess. 'You screamed just as loud as Auntie B.'

'So did you!' he retorted, 'and right in my ear. Anyway, I only screamed to keep your scream company.'

Auntie B laughed.

'How you all went on that dreadful train which turned upside down, I'll never know. Give me a nice, safe roundabout any day.'

'Roundabouts are boring,' said Benjy dismissively.

She laughed again good-naturedly and turned to me.

'What did you do Richard?'

'Nothing much. In the afternoon I took some fruit around, like you suggested.'

'Good. Were the Edwards pleased?'

'I didn't go there.'

Auntie B was looking at me, expecting an explanation.

'I took some pears to Mr Wassilewska – to Stef, over the fence.'

'Mum said we aren't allowed to do that,' said Benjy smugly.

Auntie B and Dad exchanged looks.

'So what!' I was suddenly furious.

'She did,' Benjy whined. 'Mum said . . .'

'Oh do shut up!' I growled. 'Anyway, you sneak in there all the time.'

'I don't!' he shrieked. 'I never go there. I haven't been there . . . today! Have I, Auntie B? Have I?'

'Stop it!' wailed Tess. 'Stop it, both of you. Stop it! Dad, make them stop it!'

'I think,' said Dad, jumping to his feet, 'that it's time we cut that extra-special birthday cake that I saw in the kitchen.' This year Dad had ordered the cake from a shop.

Benjy rushed out to get it and I scowled: they all encouraged him to be even more stupid than usual. He made a real performance about lighting all eight candles and dropped matches and bits of wax everywhere. I yawned when he made his wish, but when I glanced at Tess for sympathy her eyes were tightly shut and I am sure that she was wishing too. He challenged us to guess his wish but I wouldn't join in. I knew he'd only wish something stupid and I didn't want to know what it was.

Later, as I lay in bed, I wondered if Benjy had spoken the truth. I hadn't seen him in Stef's garden recently. In fact, I hadn't seen him in there since Mum went. And I was glad. I was certain that Mr Wassilewska didn't like him.

Unfortunately, I didn't have a chance to go either for several days. Then, on Saturday morning, the bell rang early and Mr Wassilewska was on our doorstep again. He had a large book in his arms. Auntie B was still in her dressing-gown and they were both embarrassed.

'Please excuse me, madam.' He backed away, hugging the book to his chest and apologising.

'No, no.' She pushed her hair back and also apologised.

'It's just the map,' he said.

'What map?' I asked tactlessly over Auntie B's shoulder, but he had turned away.

'Mr Wassilewska!' I called, but he didn't stop and didn't even look up either, as he closed the garden gate.

I hadn't meant to be rude, so I didn't see why he was offended and I wouldn't even have bothered about it if Benjy and I hadn't had a massive row that afternoon. Benjy had borrowed my stereo again, and I'd had enough. Auntie B said that she hadn't thought it mattered, because I was out of the house and so couldn't possibly have listened to any music at the time. I didn't even try to explain that that wasn't the point. She wouldn't have understood.

I just walked out angrily.

'Maybe,' I muttered on the other side of the door, 'you'd like to give him my camera as well. And my football. I'm not using them at the moment, either!'

This time I didn't ring Mr Wassilewska's bell but went round the side of the house to the steps. His chair was out, but unoccupied. I guessed that he hadn't gone far. The sun had disappeared behind the clouds and the warm day was now a dull, grey afternoon. It was chilly sitting and waiting because I had come out in a T-shirt. Then I remembered the blanket in the porch behind me. He wouldn't mind, surely.

I pulled at a corner and drew out a thick, dark brown thing, that was more like a carpet than a blanket. It looked well-used, so I wrapped it round my shoulders and settled myself back into his chair. The coarse fur tickled my chin and it smelt a bit odd, but it was warm.

I hoped that Auntie B would look out of the window and see me and feel guilty. I couldn't believe how much she'd changed. She used to be so nice to me and now she wasn't at all. And she spoilt Benjy. She let him do whatever he wanted, and there was no excuse. She'd even hinted that it might be worse for Benjy, because he'd never said goodbye to Mum, but he could have, couldn't he? If he'd really loved Mum, he'd have come down and said goodbye like the rest of us.

As I waited there the sky darkened further and a gloomy stillness settled into the garden. Along the valley before me the last slants of a white, watery light lit up the sharp, green hillsides, before the approaching rain. I stretched out my legs and huddled deeper beneath my rug. I shut my eyes and breathed in an old dusty odour. Somewhere I heard the rhythmic tap-tap-tap of wheels on rails or maybe the tread of feet along a road. And then this huge crowd of people was walking too quickly and some were stumbling and all called out to me with a single cry which I could not hear. Then I was awake again and the rain was pattering down on the dry rug. Mr Wassilewska was hurrying up the steps, shaking his umbrella and calling my name.

'Well,' he laughed, 'good job you found my old friend, before the storm.'

I glanced around, not understanding.

'My rug – my faithful old travelling friend. That rug kept me snug and dry all the way from the Russian steppe to the Persian mountains.'

'Is that where they took you then? To Persia?'

'No, no. I went to Persia, certainly, but that's not where they took me. You really want to see where they took me?' He looked at me sceptically.

'Yes! I wanted to this morning, honestly, only my aunt wouldn't let me. She never let me do anything . . .'

Mr Wassilewska listened in silence to my lies and I think we were both relieved when the pattering rain suddenly strengthened and drove us hurriedly indoors.

'There,' he said, opening up the atlas. 'Kazakhstan. *That* is where they took us.' And he drew his finger slowly back across the two pages and stopped at a black dot in southern Poland: Lvov.

'My home was there, in a small place just near.'

Even on the map the distance between the two was vast. 'Did you go all that way in the railway wagon?'

'That and others: they made us change trains on the Polish–Russian border, because the size of the track is different.'

'It must have taken days and days.'

'No. Not days: weeks. Six weeks for some of us. For others their journey was not so long.'

I did not want to understand.

'An old man died first and then a baby. Then, one morning the guards took away some men who had tried to escape and my mother would not let me look out to see what happened to them. But I heard. Then a small boy dies and, do you know – I was not so sad, for that boy had cried and cried. And with them gone there was more room, and more to drink. Every other day the train stopped, usually at some quiet station, then each wagon must send one person out to fetch this bucket of dark, hot water with bits floating in it, that they call tea. They give us that, with half a loaf of bread that we would have thrown only to our pigs. At first not everybody will drink and eat, though my mother makes me, and will not give me any of the good food that I now knew she had hidden in the sack from the woodshed. Soon, though, there are arguments and even a fight and it was not just rough people who fought. It was people whom we had visited in town, who had pianos and went to church and spoke foreign languages; they quarrelled and swore over this foul water and this sour, hard bread.'

'And what did you do, Mr Wassilewska?'

'Me? Oh. I just watched them. And scratched. Then I sleep but I must always wake and scratch some more. You have seen lice?'

'No!'

'Well, you would have seen plenty with us. Soon, we are all covered in lice: they take a walk on us like it is playtime: great fat, grey lice. It itches so badly – but I cannot cry. I am too old, my mother says, to cry about lice or about the men they take away. Josef may cry, because he is little and he does. He, however, cries more about our dog that we have left behind and my mother holds him in her arms and rocks him to and fro. Then one day, I am so angry with his snivelling that I tell him not to worry because everybody knows that Russian soldiers eat dogs! And he never cried about that again.

So that's what we do, Peter and I. We sit together, away from our families, and we scratch and watch and plan our escape: as soon as the train stops next time, we will escape.

Then, early one morning – and I thought it was morning because other people were still asleep – I look out and the landscape is different. In the far, far distance, there are mountains and Peter, who is also awake, tells me that we have passed the Ural Mountains. More people wake and we all look out and are very, very quiet and now no one says that we will be going back home. And even I, who was not a good scholar, knew that the Urals are deep inside Russia and a long, long way from Poland and from my home. We are on the far side of the Urals in another world we call Asia, the world of the endless steppe.

Already some people in the wagon have no food left and my mother, who I now realise had made secret preparations in case this happened, actually gives a little of our food to a family who is hungry. I was so angry with her, and ask why she gives them what she would not give me. She looks at me coldly and I remember how she spoke when she made me get that sack. Now she gives to strangers what I risked my life to save.'

'But she didn't mean it like that, did she?' I asked.

'No. But I did not understand that then. I was just a miserable boy. And you know what? My little brother was not so miserable as me. He starts to laugh and play and talk to everyone. He was always a very friendly boy – like your little brother.'

'Benjy isn't friendly. He's spoilt. And a nuisance.'

'So was my brother. He was a nuisance, he never stayed still. Always he was running in and out, asking questions, interfering, telling even grown-ups how to do something. When our guard comes in, Peter and I pretend not to see him but Josef chatters to this enemy in his schoolboy Russian. "Where are we going? . . . Why don't we have water to drink . . . Why can't we go home?" At first my mother is terrified that they will punish him, or take him away too. Other people also complain: "Mrs Wassilewska, please ask your son to be quiet!"

Then I notice that the situation has changed: they are using him, "Josef, run over and ask Mrs Berk if I can borrow her sewing needle." "Josef, be a good boy and play with my baby, so I can get some sleep". "Josef, look out quick and tell us what you can see!" "Josef, ask the guard for more bread, please – but don't let anyone else hear!"

Everyone loves my little brother and they stroke his golden curls and pat his cheeks that are getting thinner and thinner. They give him little presents of this and that and Mother tells him to refuse but he doesn't, and I know that she is secretly proud of him.

Sometimes, when the train is stationary, people approach it cautiously from accross the steppe. We hear their voices, in strange accents, calling softly to us. They are selling food and they strike a hard bargain. These people look so hungry and poor themselves, with their ragged clothes and grey, anxious faces, yet they are offering real food to us. Sometimes they take quite useless things like rings and pretty blouses in return.

One afternoon, when Mother is asleep, Josef, who has been watching this trade closely, tries his luck. He is holding something out: one of Mother's lipsticks. He bargains keenly. Finally he exchanges it for a piece of cheese and a bowl half full of milk. I turn away. I cannot bear to watch him drink, but I can hear him panting as he gulps it down. He does not drink it all. He comes over to see me with the milk still creamy-white around his smiling lips and he offers half to me. I drink too and for a second I'm back at home. There is a smell of baking and we watch as Mother bends down and takes the tray of biscuits from the oven. We will eat them while they are still too hot and we will cool our mouths with the fresh milk that stands on the table in the blue china jug. I can hardly bear to swallow, for then it will all be gone.

Outside, the woman bangs on the side of the wagon for the return of the bowl. Josef leans down and hands it to her and she smiles up brilliantly, with lips that are already circled in scarlet.

Now, finally, as we travel further east, and the Urals are left behind, they open the wagon doors when the train stops. They let us out. Now we can escape. "Next time," I whisper to Peter, and I've hidden my rucksack, in preparation.

But next time, when the doors are open and I can see wild flowers blooming amidst the grasses on the steppe, next time, I do not jump down and run for there is nowhere to run to. These huge, empty grasslands stretch on for ever and ever and I see nothing at all in the distance. We would never survive out there. Sometimes we think we see a small group of low tents or huts and now and then the people who come to the train are on horseback. Their eyes are the shape and colour of burnt almonds and they look at us from out of weathered, sunburnt faces and they barter in a language that no one understands. And when they've finished their trade they spur their horses and wheel around and gallop off through the flickering grass, and I watch them with longing.

Then news is passed back from wagon to wagon: we've arrived. Everybody is frantically gathering up their possessions. I peer out. I can see nothing. They must be wrong. We cannot have arrived. There is no town, no village and no road. There are not even any trees. I'm very scared. Now, I do not want to leave this train.'

'Why? I thought it was so awful . . .'

'It was. But what will come after? That we do not know, whereas I know this wagon. All I know of the world beyond the train is its earth, that I have dug into as I helped make a grave. I am used to the train: Peter and I have a corner which we call "ours". There, while others slept, I have whispered about things that I have never spoken of to anyone else. And is not "our guard" better than some others? He has not beaten any of us, yet.

The bolts go back and we blink in the chill early-morning light. We crowd around the door, but suddenly, none of us will step down. A line of carts waits at a distance. They are ox-carts and the men who walk towards us carry whips and are dressed in strange padded jackets. And beyond them there is nothing. No house, no light, not even, I realise, a horizon. I cannot see into the 'distance': it is too far or maybe I am too exhausted.

The guards take out their lists and check them. Now they smile encouragingly. "You are safe now," they say, as though they have snatched us from the jaws of wolves.

"Come!" Our guard, who has always worn medals on his chest, holds out his hands. No one moves. "Come along!" My little brother steps forward and lets himself be swung down by the cruel man on to a land that is not ours. Josef makes a little run to right and left and kicks a pebble, and turns back to smile at us like a child let free at the seaside. My mother follows him, of course, but she stumbles like an old woman. I realise for the first time that her dark chestnut hair is streaked with ugly bands of grey.

I hang back. "Come," the guard says quite gently, "you must all understand that this is a new life for you. A new chance in another land." But he looks around as though he too is a little scared.

They are sending people to the carts. Peter is sent to the second cart, Mother and Josef to the first, Peter's father to the second and then I, too, and I'm pleased: it seems to be the cart for men. I am suddenly as excited as if it were a school trip and I am to sit by my friend. I see our German teacher in that cart as well. My mother screams and runs back, and is no longer old.

"No!" she screams. "No. He may not go in that cart! He is not old enough. He is only fourteen and that is not allowed in Soviet law." They all stare at her, the men with the whips and the guards with their guns, and I stare too.

"It doesn't really matter." I say.

"No!" she cries. "He is my son. And he stays with me." She goes very close to the man with the list. "Do you not know the law?" she shouts. "Well, I know the law and I tell you that you are wrong. It is forbidden." Then she speaks in Polish to my brother. "Cry!" she hisses, "cry!" and I see her pinch the skin of his neck and he howls and howls again and the guards fling me away so that I fall at my mother's feet. My knees are so weak that I cannot walk to the first cart. I must crawl.'

'Did she really know the law?'

'No. Of course not. But she knew the Russians and she guessed what might happen.'

'What did . . . happen?'

'The second cart turned off.'

He paused and moved around the room and switched on the light, for the rain had made it very dark.

'After an hour, maybe, it turned off. There was no track that we could see, though I suppose those men could. Anyway, the driver cracked his whip and the second cart lumbered and creaked away . . .'

'Where to?'

'Later I heard that they took them to the mines, and we heard also that it was very bad. But some were not there so long. There was an accident with the dynamite and some of our men did not come back.'

He only paused for a moment and then he laughed.

'So you see, she did know best.'

I found it hard to understand the joke. Apart from Mum, the only person I'd known who'd had something happen to them was the brother of a girl in my class. He'd been knocked down on the crossing near school. And I hadn't really known him, either. But all the same . . . I didn't understand how anyone could joke about things like that.

Then I realised that I'd still got the heavy rug thing over my shoulders. I took it off and as I did so, I noticed the photo of a bear for the first time. It wasn't a very good photo, but I could see that it was of a dark-coloured bear which appeared to be fighting with a man in a soldier's uniform.

I awkwardly refolded the rug and suddenly realised with horror what I must be holding: a bearskin.

'Is that your old friend?' I asked pointing to the photo, remembering what he had said on the steps.

'Why, of course. That is my old friend Voytek. The famous soldier bear. You know about him?'

I shook my head uncomfortably. I was glad Tess wasn't with me. She's keen on animal rights and though I'm sure she'd have liked Mr Wassilewska, if she knew him, I was also sure that she would hate to learn that he'd made a bear into a rug. I wasn't particularly keen on the idea myself.

'So, I must tell you about that too, about Voytek. So much to tell. But you are not bored? No?'

'No. But . . .' I stroked the rug, nervously. 'Is this . . . is this . . . that bear?'

He looked at me in astonishment, then he began to laugh. In fact, he laughed so much and so loudly that I wondered if he really was a bit odd after all.

'You think this is the skin of that bear, Voytek?' he finally gasped with tears running down his cheeks.

'Well, isn't it?' I continued. I didn't want to be laughed at. 'I mean, I know people shoot bears in Russia and places like that, and I thought maybe you had.'

'No. Never bears: much too big and fierce. I am only a little man. I just hunted rats and lice and fleas, yes. But bears? Never. Now *that* bear, in the photo, *that* bear is

Voytek. And we found him in Persia. But my rug – that is another part of my story. Do you really want to hear about that too?'

I nodded. I wanted to hear so much and I no longer wanted to go back to the spoilt landscape of my home. I wanted to stay with Stef Wassilewska and return instead to the lost and distant territories of his past.

6

A New Chance in Another Land . . .

*H*E MADE ME GO HOME. HE INSISTED THAT I ASK permission to stay for supper and I was surprised at how readily Auntie B agreed. I thought she'd refuse or tell me to leave it till another day, but she didn't. She barely glanced up from the jigsaw which she and Benjy were doing at the kitchen table. There were grey streaks in her untidy hair and I thought how shabby and tired she looked. I was surprised that Benjy hadn't noticed. He had his arm around her neck.

'Would you like to stay there for supper?' she asked.

'Well, there's nothing for me to do here, is there?'

'Not at the moment,' she said evenly, 'but be back by nine.'

'Why?'

She looked at me then. She wasn't just shabby. She was old, too, and a nerve in her cheek twitched.

'I'd like you to be back by nine, please, Richard.'

'All right. If that'll make you happy. Auntie.'

I ran back through the rain and despised her for being so feeble. The shrubs and trees in Mr Wassilewska's overgrown garden were dripping wet, and half of it soaked on to me. I knew it was still summer but it felt like autumn already.

He was waiting for me, and began at once. He wasn't

bothered that I was wet.

'Those terrible fleas,' he laughed. 'But I'm afraid that's all I hunted in Kazakhstan. Not bears. I'm sorry to disappoint you but I wasn't a hero, even then. Now, where were we? In the ox-carts?'

So, after several hours we came to a small, drab settlement in the middle of the empty steppe. And they showed us where we were to live. I cannot believe it. It was a place for goats and sheep before and had a broken door and no window and was – about so big.'

He paced out a rectangle of maybe ten strides by ten. 'It was made of mud bricks and I could see twigs and tufts of grass in the roof. I won't go in.

My mother does, Josef follows, but runs back out holding his nose. My mother takes a scarf and ties up her hair, hiding it all away so that she is almost a stranger. She looks at me impatiently.

"Don't just stand there," she mocks. 'You heard what the guards said: this is your new chance in another land." Her voice is harsh, and though she must have been so tired, she did not stop for a moment. She wrenches a board from the door and begins to use it as a spade to clear the dung from our new house.

We are to report for work in the morning, we are told, and immediately my mother is lying again.

"No," she says to the leader of the settlement, "my elder son is not fourteen, he is only twelve, so he cannot work." She points at me and demands, "Does he *look* fourteen?"

I know that I don't, but my pride is a little hurt.

"Why did you lie?" I asked later. "I could work. Honestly, Mother."

"I know," she says, rubbing her hands across her dirty face. "But who will look after Josef if we both work?" Then she is on her hands and knees again trying to clean that wretched place.

But, do you know, by nightfall, while others are still weeping, we have a sort of bed made up in there, with sheets and blankets, and as soon as I lie down, I sleep. When I wake I suspect that we are not alone. There is a very strong smell and it is one I almost know. Stranger still, people are shoving and shifting about near me, and I can't remember if I'm still on the train or not. Then one of these stinking guests opens her mouth and says "Baaa . . ." It is the goats! They have come back in through the broken door and they are eating the corner of a sheet!

My poor mother leaps up screaming. We chase them out like madmen. When my mother examines that spoilt sheet, she really cries. "It was linen," she sobs: it had been a wedding gift, long ago . . .

She sits on the bit of wall outside and sobs uncontrollably over the chewed sheet. I'm scared of her tears and wander off. When I look back, Josef has come out and put his arms around her and together they stare across the grasslands to where the great sun rises up over the steppe.

So, day by day we learn to live this new life. Mother goes to work early and her first job is to make bricks from the mud. Later, she will help with the potatoes.

For the moment Josef and I are free, and for me, it is very strange. There is a school, we hear, over in the next settlement, but nobody suggests to send me, and I don't want to go. I was good enough in school in Lvov, but no more, and I hate to read and write. Mathematics? That's not so bad, but literature, poetry, oh I hate it: always so gloomy. Now I'm glad that I'm free and the days are getting warmer. There are flowers on the steppe: a blue iris and yellow wormwood flowered amongst the grass which was beginning to grow again after the long winter. In other places where the ground is still wet, the grass is already knee-high. We must go to get water from a small, marshy pond with a few trees around it. The sides sloped down and once I saw two long-legged birds wading amongst the reeds at the water's edge. It was as if Creation had started to make a gentle country scene and then had got disheartened and had given up.

Out there, on the steppe, it is one of my tasks to fetch water, and I don't mind it. Another of my duties is to collect dung to burn. Each day Josef and I go out with that sack from the woodshed and we collect pats of dried manure. Some we burn at once, for cooking; whatever is left over we start to make into a store "for later". Mother says that we must collect as much as we can. There were a few other Polish children around and we went out in a group with some of the Kazakh children as well. We wandered all over the steppe and would have got lost many times, except for the local children. The little ones squabble about "who saw 'what' first" – and some of them make dirty jokes about it and I'm quite shocked because I have never heard anything like that at home, so I don't want to laugh. But Josef laughs loudest of all, and soon makes the rudest jokes. And in the end I smile too. As payment for her work Mother gets flour and milk and sometimes cheese and very occasionally a scrap of meat, mutton or goat, I think. The amounts are very small and we are getting thinner and thinner and also as sunburnt as the people who live here. Now they no longer tease me about my fine rich man's skin. The weather is getting hotter and soon we sleep outside at night.

One day Josef and I are waiting in front of the hut: the dung fire is burning and I have my boy-scout kettle on it boiling merrily. I'm quite proud of myself. I have already made the flour into little flat cakes. When we see Mother in the distance, we will fry them, well, cook them, as we have no fat. Josef sees her first but dust is rising up from her feet: she is running. He runs to her, but I stay squatting by the fire, blowing in the dung to keep it burning. She has had a letter. The chief of the settlement has just given it to her, though it had arrived at the post office a few days ago: we think he reads all the letters first. It is from my oldest brother, from Edward.

My mother's hand is shaking. She cannot read it, but gives it to me.

"My dearest Mother and brothers and sisters, greetings to you all from the North. I am well here and am working in the forest. I have had news of you from Stanislawa who is still on the farm and though she has written to you, I will tell you too. She is expecting a baby in October – now that is good news, isn't it? Have you had news of Father? I have had none. We are all well and soon it will be spring here, people say. May God keep us all safe – Your loving son and brother."

My voice shakes so much that I can hardly read it either. Mother tells us that Edward is in a labour camp far in the north. We are very quiet that evening and we make up our beds early. Tonight, although she is so tired, my mother hasn't fallen asleep. When I awake a little later, scratching because of the lice, I see that she has got up and is sitting out alone in the night. She is gazing up to the stars above. In that half-light, I cannot see the lines that now spoil her tired face. She is almost beautiful.

"I hope," she says, when I touch her arm, "all we can hope is that wherever they are, they too can still look up and see the stars."

Do you know, until that moment, whenever I thought about my family, I had always thought about us all together, as we had been in our new house, even though I knew that it wasn't like that any more. That night when she and I looked up at the stars, I began to understand what my mother must have realised all the time: that we might never be together there again; and that we might never all look up to the stars again. It frightened me but I did not dare ask her about it, not that night. Instead, I thought about what the letter had not said. It had said nothing about my middle brother, Jan, and nothing of my little sister, Maria. And what had Edward meant when he said that, for him, spring had yet to come? Here, on the steppes of Kazakhstan, it was summer and was getting even hotter. How far north was he that it was still winter? And what was a labour camp? That night when I lay down to sleep again I took care not to disturb Josef. Let him at least sleep soundly.

And those goats, you know, were not our only visitors. Often, when Josef and I returned from the steppe we would find some of our neighbours sitting in our hut fingering our possessions. After their first visit, Mother tried to keep as much as possible hidden away, but still they came. They were fascinated by what we had, and angry with us, I think, for having it. I did not understand that then. They had been told so many contradictory things about us Poles: first, that we were starving and wretched in our own land and so had begged to be taken to safety and prosperity in Russia. Later, they had been told that we, as "rich people", were criminals because we had become rich while others starved. We were the enemies of the Soviet people. Now, these poor confused neighbours looked at what little we had: our leather boots and shoes, our coats and linen sheets, my mother's pretty dresses, even my little camping kettle, and they were almost as confused as we were. They thought us rich, while we felt desperately poor. But some of them liked us and they all liked Josef very much. They loved his curly fair hair, his fun, his friendliness, his jokes, and then, when he fell ill, I began to understand these people in a different way.

The illness appeared in midsummer. All around us people were falling ill – babies first, then an old Polish man, then several people from one family nearby. Josef had actually played with their son. And there is no medicine, no help. The illness always took the same form: a raging fever and terrible diarrhoea, streaked with blood

– and this in houses with no toilet. And remember, it is in summer, so you can imagine the flies and the dirt and danger. I remember that Mother boiled all our water, covered up all our food, but even then, it was impossible. We woke in the night to find great black flies crawling along our cracked lips. When Josef fell ill, he faded like a plucked flower, tossed down under the scorching sun. My mother got permission to stop working. She nursed him day and night and told me that I must go to work in the brick factory in her place. That first evening, I thought I could not walk home because my arms and legs ached so badly after the heavy work. But, of course, I managed it and little by little it got a bit better. Even, I began to like it. I am not so bored. There were people to talk to and there was Jana, this beautiful Kazakh girl with eyes that were green and skin that was the colour of wheat, and dark straight brows. And her arms, I remember, were rounded and strong.'

He smiled, but not at me, and I too could imagine that girl, toiling under the glaring sun, laying endless rows of bricks out to dry, and intercepting his stealthy glances from under the brim of her sunhat. I noticed with bewilderment that outside, it had stopped raining. I had almost expected to see the burnt grasslands of the steppe.

'What happened to Josef?'

'Josef?'

'Your little brother, who was so ill . . .'

'Of course. That is when I learn more about my neighbours. One of them brought a man from another settlement secretly to our hut at night. He is a doctor, he says, or was, and he too has been sent out here, as a punishment. He has come from Moscow and has been here nearly eight years, a Russian, not a Kazakh: a doctor, without a hospital, a man with no future. But he saved Josef for us. He gave my mother some cornflour and a little salt and told her that she must make this into a thin, salty soup for Josef and that she must feed him this, a spoonful at a time, day and night, and that she must bathe his head and body to try to keep him cool – and this she did, day and night, for two weeks.

And she saved him – they saved him, my mother and this doctor. She tried to thank him, but he would take none of our things. It was enough, he said, to have been allowed to use his skills again, and for so nice a family, for such a brave patient as Josef. We liked him, very much and he began to visit us at weekends; Josef called him "Uncle", though he always called my mother Mrs Wassilewska. It was he who warned us about the coming winter and who found us wood to repair the door. He was a kind friend and I thought nothing of it until one day I overheard some Polish women talking about us at the brickworks.'

'So you stayed on working there?'

'Yes. As summer progressed Mother found work in the potato fields, so that Josef could go too, as soon as he was strong enough. At first, she had to carry him on her back. Later she persuaded them to let her look after one of the flocks of goats and sheep but I stayed on at the brickworks all summer. I liked it. I got some food as payment and, of course, I had fallen in love. For the first time.'

'With Jana?'

'Naturally with Jana. Who else should I love? She was the prettiest of the girls. But it was a very difficult love affair for someone as inexperienced as me.'

'Why?'

'Well, she was older than me – maybe seventeen. I don't exactly know. Then, all the boys are in love with her: Poles, Kazakhs, Russians – we all love Jana. And, she does not love me – does not even talk to me, and finally – what you say? – last but not least, she is engaged to marry someone else. But I am not defeated. Oh no. When you are fourteen – and in love, you cannot imagine defeat. I think: in time she will love me, because I love her so much. I secretly look in my mother's mirror to see if my moustache is growing. And when it isn't, I think it is the terrible heat, or maybe the fleas. Maybe I have scratched my beard away for ever!

So I make my bricks but I watch her all the time and sometimes I help her to make her bricks. Then one day in autumn, she is not there. Nor the next and I ask, "Where is Jana?" and you know what they say?'

I replied without thinking: 'That she's dead?'

'No, no. Well, not quite but as good as, as far as I'm concerned. She's married. And I see her with a tall, handsome man: a soldier back on leave. The next day, she returns to work, red-eyed from crying all night, I suppose, and I think, "Ha. So he's a no-good bum. Now she will look at a good guy like me, even if I'm as thin as a plucked chicken."'

'Did she?'

'No. She is crying because her new young husband has returned to the front to fight against the Germans who are now attacking Russia, we hear. And that is when I first hear the older women talking about us. "Don't waste your pity on young Jana," one says to another, "she'll soon find a new man for herself. Look at that Mrs Wassilewska, it didn't take her long."

At first I did not understand, then I was angry, but not with those foolish women. I was angry with my mother!'

'But – but . . .'

'Exactly. It was just gossip: idle, cruel gossip, but I was a fool and believed them and I should have known better.'

'So what happened?'

'Nothing, at first. I did not have the courage to ask my mother, or to warn her what people were saying, but I was very unpleasant to her and very rude to the good doctor.'

I shifted restlessly and fiddled with my shoes.

'I've talked already too much', said Mr Wassilewska, noticing my discomfort, 'and you're bored. I'm sorry. You must be very hungry and I haven't given you the supper I promised.'

His kitchen wasn't like ours. In fact, it wasn't like any kitchen I'd ever been in, and I couldn't help staring. It was as though I had stepped into the pages of a children's fairy-tale.

'You like it?' he asked.

I nodded. I did like it and I remembered what he had told me about the home that he had left behind. No wonder he spent so much time in this kitchen. It was beautiful: a different world, of carved wood and brightly painted tiles and intricate shelves full of plates and cups and china figures. An old-fashioned white enamelled stove stood against one wall. There were cushions and curtains and mats and tapestries, all embroidered in a rainbow of bright colours.

'Did you do all this, Mr Wassilewska?'

'The woodwork, yes, most of it. I hate to write – that you know, words are such fiddly, awkward things, but I am good with my hands in other ways. I like to carve. And the sewing – that is not my work, that I buy – in Polish bazaars, from other Polish people. There are many, many Polish people here in England. This,' he pointed to a tapestry of Christ on the Cross, 'this, the wife of a friend made me as a present. The same lady who made the poppyseed cake. Those cushions, I ordered from a shop in Poland. They are new.'

'But . . .'

'You want to know "why?" don't you?'

I nodded again.

'I tell you that too, if I can. But first we have soup. Not Polish soup – but English soup – no, I lie, I think Scottish soup, and out of a can too. I'm not a cook.'

We ate quickly, and almost in silence. We were both impatient.

'You know about winters on the steppe?' he asked suddenly.

'Not really.'

'Then I tell you, and you will understand. We knew, of course, that winter was coming, but that first autumn was long. We have seen huge flocks of birds flying south, but it has not snowed yet. There were heavy frosts at night, and in shady places, such as the pool where I get the water, the frost and ice cling all day long. In the early morning the wind sings through the thin, frozen reeds. In open places it is still sunny at midday and we think it is not so bad. We'll manage, we say, but soon it is so cold that my hands have cracked and I must bind them up in rags. Soon the ground is frozen all day long. Suddenly we can find no more fuel, the dung, the odd stick, the long grass, all is frozen. We can't pick anything up. The frost grasps more tightly than any hand.

Already we are wearing all our clothes. The Kazakh people, some of them, have thick felt over-boots, but not us. My boots are falling apart. My feet have grown, though I cannot imagine how, when I am always starving. Each morning before I leave the house I must tie them round with strips of cloth. Taking my boots off is not good – sometimes I cry from pain, but in silence. Sometimes, I do not take them off at all but crawl straight into bed and hope my mother will not see. When they tell me that the brick factory will now close until spring, I'm glad, until they tell me that I will get no more "pay" in the form of food. I protest. This time my mother says, "Be quiet" – she is afraid that if I make a fuss they will send me to the mines, now I'm older. And it is not just my feet that have grown. I'm taller too, as tall as she is. I've seen the job I want, the perfect job: it is to look after the pigs. Now that is a much better job than making bricks.'

'It sounds disgusting. Why's it better?'

'Think,' he said. 'What do pigs eat?'

'Everything – don't they?'

'Exactly – not like sheep. Who wants to eat grass?'

'You don't mean . . .'

'Oh yes I do! I *must* get that job if I'm not to starve. I was learning. I'm not quite so stupid. I give the foreman my watch – and he gives me the job. And each day, I bring home a little something from the pig's trough—'

'From the trough?'

'Oh yes!' He smacked his lips together, and enjoyed my horror. 'You've never been hungry, have you?' he said at last. 'And I tell you another thing – pigs are warm. And that brings us back to winter. So I'm going to work each day – maybe an hour's walk, and if it is windy, nearly two hours. For the wind howls all day and all night now. And it is wind like – like the hurricane of '87 when all the trees blew down – but on the steppe it is a bitter, biting wind. And it screams as though it too is hungry. It has already snowed a bit and one evening when I look out of the sty, I'm not at all keen to go home. I would have liked to stay with the pigs, but my mother has told me I must return so that Josef will not be left alone too long. It is a long, cold walk and home will be so much colder than the sty – so I wait a bit. Maybe the wind will drop. It doesn't. It strengthens. When I finally set out, it is snowing again. Halfway home it is snowing a lot, but I keep on. I know which way to go, because I look at my boy-scout's compass, and I know that our house is only five hundred yards from the hollow where there are the trees and reeds and the frozen pool. Only they are not there, that night. The snow is so thick that I cannot see anything. Nothing at all and I stumble: one of the bands that ties my shoes on has broken. I bend down to mend it and I cannot even open my eyes – I try very hard to concentrate. I think: Stefan, just stand still and open your eyes and see where you are. I cannot. The snow presses down on my face. I try to brush it away and I drop the compass. The wind is dragging the breath from my throat and I feel dizzy.

Then I'm scared. I turn round, to go back, but my footprints have vanished. All around this storm of snow roars over me and, little by little, I realise with surprise that it is not really cold at all: the dreadful pain in my toes and feet has gone. And I think, well – I'll just rest up – for a moment – sleep it out, and when it clears – then I'll find my way back. I look for my watch – then remember that I don't have it. But I can hear something ticking. I feel a little odd and wonder if I am imagining it, but no, definitely, I can hear it. Tick tick, tick tick. Then maybe a cat mewing. Poor thing, I think. I'm sorry for it, but not for myself because, of course, I'm beginning to freeze to death, though I don't realise it. But then I hear it again "tick, tick". I make one last struggle towards that noise.

It is Josef. It is he who saved my life, like little Hansel in the story. I was in fact almost home. But the blizzard had covered the hut, as it had covered everything. I would have frozen to death within twenty steps of safety. Josef had tied one end of a rope to his wrist and another to the handle of the door and he had come out into the storm and was banging a stone against the bottom of a tin plate. Every now and then he called my name into the wind, and it was that which I had heard. The doctor was right, Josef was brave.

I do not remember how we got back in, but we did follow that rope, hand over hand, and Josef managed to get the fire going again. But we could not close the door properly. A heap of snow had already streamed in and was of course too heavy for us to shift. The whole hut was covered over. It was buried, and there is no doubt that that's what I'd have been, dead and buried, if Josef had not risked his life for me. He and I stayed alone in the hut for two days. Mother had had to stay at her work with the goats and we were not reunited until the villagers dug us out. It was, I learnt, one of the great dangers of the steppe. It was a place where one can vanish without trace. And not just in the winter blizzards, either. In summer, when the grass is high and the pollen is blowing like a thick white mist, then, too, you could lose your way and die of heat and thirst.

That night the whole settlement was buried, and for several weeks no one could go out to work. We are all imprisoned, all over again, and it is then that I start to do two things. Often, when we talk of home, I start to remember that house. I begin in the kitchen with the tiles – for maybe that was where I was most often. I recall that room, corner by corner and inch by inch. I try to remember every detail of each picture on every tile. I lie on the bed which is a heap of grass and reeds which we had collected in the summer, and my mind drifts back. And I think about it so carefully that I know it in my head, what it is really like. I know the colour of the bluebells on the tiles by the sink. I know exactly how the buttonholes in that quilt had been worked by my grandmother.

And of course, later, when I have the chance to build a new house, I'm not interested in the house that the architect has drawn so nicely. Oh no. I must build the house that is already in my head.'

'So *this* house is the new house where your family was before the war.'

'No. *This* is the house that was in my head. And that is not the same.'

He was pushing the crumbs of bread carefully together and squeezing them into a ball.

'You said you started two things, Mr Wassilewska, when you were snowed in.'

'Yes, I did. I also started to carve. With my boy-scout knife, I began. And you know what I carve? Ice, of course. And I can do it. I, who hated to write, who was all thumbs and ink-blots and wrong letters, I can make things that are not words, with my hands.' He pointed proudly at the carved shelves. 'But, of course, there was no wood to spare on the steppe. When the ice melted, then I carved stone.'

'Oh goodness,' I said, suddenly catching sight of the clock on one of the shelves, 'I mustn't be late. Auntie B said not after nine.'

It was five to, and now I didn't want to be late. When he opened the door I almost expected that a wall of white snow would tumble in but there was only the lingering scent of summer rain and the soft splash of drops falling from the leaves.

On the step I turned back.

'Mr Wassilewska? Did she, you know, love him?'

He stopped at the railing and laid his hands on the wet black iron.

'I do not know. But yes, now that I am old, I wonder if she did—'

I ran down his garden and squeezed back through the fence, because I did not want to be late.

7

Dreams of Freedom

THAT NIGHT I DREAMT OF A HILLSIDE IN ITALY. I
almost reached the balcony where I knew she'd be
because I'd heard her voice whispering down from the
warm, sweet shade of the vine. I struggled towards her,
but the rope didn't reach that far and though I called and
called she never heard me and I could not climb the steps
to find her.

I suppose I overslept. The house was empty that
morning and Auntie B had left a note by my breakfast
place. 'Back at 2 p.m. Love B.' I was pleased. That gave
me at least three hours, maybe four. I'd already spotted
Mr Wassilewska. I knew he was expecting me because
he'd put the second chair out. It was a hot day of brilliant
sunshine, after the rain. They'd probably gone swimming,
they'd discussed it the evening before. I'd noticed that
Auntie B liked days out, whereas Mum never had. Mum
had always talked about doing things, but we never did.
We always stayed in. Auntie B would toss things into her
old Citroën and be off in a matter of minutes.

'Good morning,' said Mr Wassilewska cheerfully, as I
approached. 'How about trying to reach the sun and the
desert today? I've had enough of snow and anyway, I
think you will enjoy to hear about the bear, Voytek.'

He pointed to Persia on the old atlas, and ran his

fingers over a range of brown mountains in the east: the Hamadan Mountains.

'That,' he said, 'is where we found the bear, Voytek. In these mountains.'

'I don't understand. How could you be thousands of miles away on the steppe of Kazakhstan and then suddenly in Persia? How did you get there, Mr Wassilewska?'

'By the railway again! We go by rail to Tashkent, then to the town of Krasnovodsk, which is in the west, by the Caspian Sea. From there we sail over the sea to Pahlevi in Persia.' He pointed it all out on the map.

'I can see that that's the route, I mean, how could you *leave* the steppe? Did you escape? What *really* happened?'

He shut the atlas sharply.

'It was very complicated,' he said. 'It was politics. Politics and war, and too difficult to explain to you. But we left.'

He didn't look at me and it sounded like somebody else speaking. For the first time I didn't believe him and I didn't know what to say. We sat uncomfortably side by side and continued to stare out over the tops of the trees in awkward silence.

'What about this bear?' I said at last.

'I'm sorry.' His voice was unsteady. 'I'm sorry. I'm old and old men are foolish too. Of course it is not too complicated to explain to you. You're right. It is just *hard* to explain. For *me*, it is very hard, and very painful.'

'You don't have to, Mr Wassilewska. I mean, not if you don't want to.'

'But I do want to. So, let me try: that first winter in Kazakhstan – my winter of love and blizzards, that was 1940–41, yes? So, we are still in spring and in the summer of 1941. And what a summer: I never knew it could be so hot – 45 degrees in the shade: we joked that you must drink fast or the water will evaporate before you have swallowed it. In summer, those racing winter winds are burning hot, like tongues of flame from a stove. After the spring thaw they dry everything up. The land, the grasses, the animals, the potato crop, the rivers, even we dry up. I'm growing tall, but not plump and strong like my brothers were back home. I'm a scarecrow, a dried-up branch, all ankles and wrists sticking out of ragged clothes.

But I'm not dead yet, oh no, I'm more like the dried reeds which still rustle along the edges of the vanished streams. One spark and I am on fire with anger, if anything annoys me. And everything annoys me: the lice, the dirt, the dust, the boredom, the closeness of the hut, the food which is always the same, my mother, my brother – especially my brother. Josef is making new friends. They call for him to play, Kazakh and Polish children and the few Russian children whose parents are also in exile. He is going to school now, and learning Russian. He says he likes it. He is forgetting his Polish. My mother is so pleased, she says that at least he is safe in school! Safe! I'm furious. How can he be "safe" in the hands of our enemies? He learns songs about "Russian heroes" and walks home singing them. Can you imagine it?

We have also received a few more letters, both from Edward in the prison camp in Starobelsk and from distant family still around Lvov. It is not good news. The Germans have pushed the Russians back and have entered Lvov. It is in ruins. No one has heard news of my father, but there are rumours that many Polish officers may have been murdered. I do not believe these rumours, but my mother does and we quarrel about it often. She never speaks of him now. Nor will she speak about my sisters, Stanislawa and Maria. We think they are on the farm but we have no sure news. We have not heard any more news about Stanislawa's expected baby.

Then we get a parcel from my grandmother's farm. There is sugar, salt, semolina, soap and garlic, but there is no letter. The parcel has already been opened, it seems, so maybe a letter has gone. My mother makes us a pudding which tastes of garlic and soap. Josef laughs and says that it is the most delicious thing he has ever eaten. We all enjoy it and none of us mentions my little sister, Maria, though we all know that semolina pudding with nutmeg on top was her favourite food. How can Mother bear to eat it, I ask myself. How can she still smile at Josef and not weep about Maria?'

'That's like Benjy,' I said. 'He never, ever says anything, either.'

'We are all different. Now, I understand that better. Then, I did not understand at all. So, I was always angry, so angry. At work, I quarrel. I'm always in trouble, even in fights. They tell my mother that now I am fifteen, I must go to the mines, and I'm pleased! I have to go, to be a man, amongst men. I'm tired of women and children and old people. If I am to survive, I begin to think that I must be free from my family. But before I can be sent to the mines – because my mother again protests and delays things – before I leave, we hear this rumour of freedom.

The Russians have been persuaded to take their hands from our throats, we hear. Germany, which had attacked Russia in 1940, has been pressing steadily eastwards. Stalin, who you will remember was leading the Russians, has, it is rumoured, now made an agreement: he will "pardon" us Poles, who are "criminals" and the "enemies" of the people. Now, in 1941, it is rumoured that we are to be "pardoned" and set free: we may leave, and form a new army and fight *with* the Russians and their allies, the English, and the Americans, *against* the Nazi armies of Germany.

At first I hardly care believe this rumour: if it is true I will finally be able to leave this place. Suddenly, I am wild with excitement. I won't just leave. I will also have the chance to be a soldier. Some of the older people are not so excited. Their joy has turned to dark anger: "We never *were* criminals!" they protest. "How dare Stalin offer us a pardon! It is he who should be begging us for pardon, for snatching us from our homes and our country."

I don't care. I only want to leave. I think of it all day and at night I dream of freedom. Sometimes I think that being there in that hut was worse than being in a prison; at least in prison you long to join the world outside. For me, the world outside was the steppe and it was something that I hated.

I suppose I never learnt to adapt in the way that Josef did and I was jealous of him. I can remember one afternoon clearly: he was picking the irises which grew on the steppe in the early summer. He was going to try and sell them. With the flowers in his hand he pointed up to the flocks of storks migrating northwards again and he said that they were beautiful and that he would look out for them next spring. I was so angry with him. How dare he like anything about this place! I knocked the flowers from his hand and stamped them into the dust, and told him that he was a stupid little fool.

For Josef had not only learnt to like the steppe, he had also learnt to live there. His "business", which he had begun when he traded that lipstick on the train, grew and flourished. When we needed to sell any of our possessions for food, Josef always did it. He made the best bargains. He was so charming that people allowed themselves to be tricked. He also bought and sold by himself. You remember that I called him a thief? Well, it was true. He stole all the time: some potatoes here, a handful of flour there, a few nails, and once a chicken which wandered in front of our house. And my mother said nothing, for we depended on his help. Little by little he made up a small bag of nails and that he exchanged for a French book, I remember. Then he sold the book at the market and did very well.'

'Why did anyone want a French book in Kazakhstan?' I asked.

'For rolling cigarettes, of course! It was such nice, fine paper.' Mr Wassilewska laughed.

'Such a little thief, he was. I often wondered what our father would have said, but of course, he never knew. The secret police even arrested Josef, but always let him go. I think he must have made them laugh too. It was a new world, as the guard had said, and Josef understood that better than me. He thought of ways to live there. I thought of nothing but how to escape from it.

So, you can imagine, there was excitement and unrest all over the settlements that autumn. Occasionally Mother or I went into the next town. There, already, were a few men who had come back from the labour camps in the north, where spring comes so late. They told terrible tales of men worked to death and then left in frozen piles because their bodies could not be buried until the thaw. My mother would not listen to them, and tried to prevent me from hearing such things. But I sought out those men. I wanted to know.

Finally we hear news of my brother Edward. He has been freed and is on his way south to us. My mother begins to wait. At night she cannot settle down to sleep, but must go out, just once more, to see if he is coming. I often see her on the edge of the steppe, straining her eyes to catch a glimpse of him, coming through the autumn grasslands. Once, she is sure and calls to us, but it was a mirage, a trick of the light on a misty autumn morning, and I think I see the shadow of despair in her eyes.

And she's not the only one to see a mirage. Some of the men who have arrived are so changed that their own children do not recognise them and creep from them in fear. There are men who are now white-haired and gaunt, with cold, sad eyes, who have seen and done things that they dare not speak of to wives and children.

I do not want to wait for Edward. I must leave. I must go and fight. It is becoming unbearable for me, trapped in the cruel intimacy of that hut. And it is not only that: I dread spending another winter on the steppe. This time, I do not think that we can all survive. We have no stores now and almost nothing left to sell. The Kazakh people around us are also becoming poorer and poorer as the war continues. They do not have enough themselves and certainly nothing extra for us. We are weaker too. We must move on. Every evening, when she returns, I urge my mother to leave. She refuses. Suppose Edward arrives and finds his family gone? "Then he can follow," I say.

"What if he is ill too?" she asks.

"Will you be happier," I ask cruelly, "if all four of us freeze to death next winter?"

We quarrel bitterly and Josef runs between us, seeking to make peace.

In the end, she gives in. We pack. She leaves a letter for Edward with neighbours. It is already November. Snow is blowing in the wind and the ground is frozen. Josef has a cough, my mother has trouble with her eyes. We leave most of our things with people who are staying behind. Josef cries when he says goodbye to his school-friends. They promise to write. Once more we are climbing up into unheated, and uncomfortable wagons, but this time it is different. There are no barking dogs at our heels, and no guards with bayonets drawn. The chief man from the settlement has come to see us and a few others off. He shakes my mother's hand and kisses Josef. I think he almost envies us and says something to me about visiting after the war! I stare at him and pretend I have not understood, and I keep my hands in my pockets.

We are starting out with almost no food. Many, who had arrived with us, will never be returning. Some who are leaving have buried their children on the steppe, whereas others who are returning have now received news of children who might be safe, back in Poland. It will be a difficult journey back. People will often tell you that suffering unites; now, I think that it divides us, one from another.

Then I notice that the doctor has come to see us off. "Why have you come?" I ask him rudely.

"To give you this," he replies gently, "and to wish you a safe journey." He hands me a parcel, something wrapped in cloth. I will not take it, so Josef does. For a moment he clings to the doctor's hand, then he skips off with the other children in the wagon. When I look again the doctor has walked away. He is standing by himself, shielding his eyes against the flat, white light of the steppe. He waves as the train moves and my mother is very quiet.'

'What was in the parcel?'

'Tea. Several pounds of good-quality tea. I cannot imagine what he had to do to get it for us.'

'But why should he give you tea?'

'In that land of nothing, tea was like gold. Better than gold. He knew that we could sell it along the way. That tea will save my life.

We are travelling for days on end and all the time more and more people are crowding on the train. It is very cold, although we are packed in tight. People are beginning to fall ill. Some say it is typhus, others that it is influenza. Maybe this journey back is even worse, for we are now all so weak. At first we do not notice that Josef is ill. He does not complain. Then, suddenly he is no longer scrambling over the tops of everyone's luggage. He lies silently all day with his burning head resting in Mother's lap. Sometimes he tries a laugh, but his throat is so sore that he can barely swallow. At some stations guards are patrolling the trains taking off those who are sick. Mother is terrified that they will take Josef. We have heard stories of Russian hospitals, of sick people washed in cold water and left in unheated wards. We hide him, because we know that he is more likely to die in a hospital.

Then someone reports a sick boy in our carriage and the guards return. "It is nothing," Mother protests, "just a bad cold, maybe pneumonia, and nobody else can catch that. He is no danger." They will not listen. They make us get off, Mother, with Josef in her arms, and I with the bits of luggage. Once again we are stranded, cast like splintered driftwood upon an unfriendly shore.

For me, maybe that is my moment of greatest despair when I saw the train go on without me. Now I'm terrified that perhaps I will never, ever be able to leave the Soviet Union. I watch the carriages of single men go by. They are not tied down by their families; they are free to go and fight! Will I be trapped like the doctor, a forgotten man in a forgotten place? I cannot bear to think about it.

We discover that we are in a town in Uzbekistan and we stay there for two weeks. All the time my mother is nursing Josef. The representatives of the Polish Army who are looking after the families en route find us a room with several other people who are also waiting to continue their journey of escape. My mother exchanges some tea for medicines and strengthening food for Josef. I spend all my time on the streets, queueing for everything that we need. I don't mind so much. For the first time I'm hearing news of the war and news of what is happening in Poland. It is not good news, but to me those streets in that town in Uzbekistan taste of freedom and the world beyond. In the evenings I must force myself to return to our cramped room that smells of women and sick children and old, dirty clothes.

For the first time I discover that the war is being fought all over Europe and that France is occupied. I cannot wait to join the army. I have spoken to men who have fought the Germans on Polish soil in 1939. Each day I ask Josef if he still is not better, and at last he says he is. He is still very weak, but well enough to travel. Now I am busy with permits and I queue for three days to get train tickets. We stand on the platform for most of the day. Soon I am feeling guilty, Josef has fainted. Maybe it was too soon: a few more days and he would have been much stronger.

"You *are* all right, aren't you?" I ask. I have him in my arms. He is very light for a big boy of ten. His blue eyes have faded. "You're sure you're all right?" He nods. "I'm fine," he whispers. "And I'm going to be a soldier too!" We smile at each other. He knew what would please me. More and more people are pushing their way on to the platform. We are all listening for the train.

Again, I hear the silence of a crowd as we all hold our breath. We have felt the distant rumble of the train. People start to push. The train which comes in is already very crowded. I have the tickets in my pocket but I know it will be a struggle. I put Josef down beside my mother. I have the bags in my hands. People are fighting their way forward. The guards cannot keep control. I feel behind me: the tea is safely there in my rucksack. If there is a problem with a guard at the last minute, it should help buy us our places. Somebody is screaming and has fallen. I'm not going to fall. I brace myself. I *will* get a place on the train. As it grinds to a halt there is a stampede. I'm so tightly packed against a door that I cannot open it, but I do, in the end. I have lost sight of Mother and Josef. I decide to climb aboard. Once on the train, I will surely be able to see them, and help them up too. Anyway, the crowd sweeps me on and I have no free hand because of the bags. It would be hard to turn back. I stumble over the iron step but strong hands from above grab me and haul me clear. Outside, the crowd roars. I hear his shrill voice, once more. "Stefan! Wait for us! Stefan!"

I want to help them. When I manage to turn round Mother is at the door of the wagon. People have pulled her up too, but she is struggling against them. Josef is not with her. I'm trying to keep a small space free in the corner for the three of us. I cannot go back and help, because I might lose this place. Just then the train shunts the wagons and one crashes against another and the crowd howls like a beast disturbed. I watch in horror. Some people fall while others are still scrambling up. I watch my mother turn away from me and step back down into that crowd . . .'

He was breathing heavily, gasping in great gusts of breath as though he was suffocating.

I thought I understood why he had not wanted to tell me this.

'And . . . you never saw them again, did you, Mr Wassilewska?'

He shook his head. Tears were running down his cheeks. He leant back in his chair and looked away down the valley.

'All I do . . . all I did for them, was to push our bags out through the windows of the carriage. And I do not even know if they found them.'

We were quiet for a long time, he and I.

Finally he got up and fetched the old rug and held it in a bundle in his arms.

'It was on that train, which was travelling on to Krasnovodsk, that I got this rug . . .' His voice trailed away and I watched his shaking hands mechanically smoothing down the hairs on the rug, trying to lay them straight, again and again.

'Shall I go?' I asked.

'No,' he said, in a voice that was frail and fearful. It was the first time that I had heard him speak so hopelessly and so feebly and I couldn't bear to hear it.

I went down to the pool and stared into the water at the

white clouds which were caught there between the reeds. I remembered how we had parted: that she hadn't turned back and that she had never even waved goodbye.

8

On the Shore

*E*VENTUALLY, I HEARD MR WASSILEWSKA'S CHAIR CREAK and the door into his house open and shut, but I didn't go back until he called me. He'd made coffee and opened a packet of biscuits. When he offered these to me his voice was as steady as it always was and I accepted gratefully. 'At that moment,' he continued, 'I had nothing. Not only had I lost them, but I had lost everything from my former life: my ragged clothes, such as they were, a few blankets and sheets, a tin plate or two, they were all gone. I had nothing but my rucksack on my back and the remains of the tea which the doctor had given to us.

I leant back, steadying myself in my corner against the jarring motion of the train, and for a few moments I was wildly, wonderfully excited. I'd done it: I'm free, I tell myself, well, almost free. I am a young man amongst other men and we are all travelling towards our freedom. Now, no one can prevent me from doing what I want to do. Nobody can tease me and treat me like a child. There is no one to know too much about me, to doubt and contradict me, which is what families always seemed to do. I have longed to be free of my family and my desire was as guilty as it was unspoken, but now it has happened. And after all, what is to stop them catching the very next train? When we next meet, I tell myself, it will be very different. Then, the only child amongst us will be Josef. They will treat me with respect and interest. When we next meet, I will have fought for them and for our homeland and I will have helped to win them both back.

I look around at the other people in the wagon. Are they going to join the Polish Army too? As I look more carefully at my companions my excitement cools a little. Are we really the people to fight for anything any longer? Near me is a man who has lost several of his fingers to frostbite. I overhear him explaining that he was in the logging camps in Siberia. At one time he was dragging the huge, sodden tree-trunks out of the half-frozen rivers. Will he ever fight again? Two women beside me have lice on their necks and in their hair. One of them scratches and gets one of the vermin between her fingers and crushes it neatly against the button of her coat. I hear the small sound as its body splits, but they carry on their conversation. And do you know what they are discussing? Recipes – how they had made their gooseberry jam before the war! There are young men amongst us, but they are pitiably weak. Sometimes they have to help each other to their feet and their skin is stretched over their cheekbones like badly made masks. I bury my face in my hands and try to feel my own skin. Am I like that?

People are already encroaching on my space in my corner. I protest. I tell them to keep off. I have saved it specially for my family.

"What family?" asks the woman with the lice.

"My mother and my brother, who is ill," I explain.

She looks all round the carriage and then back at me. I know and understand her expression. She doesn't believe me and she is right. I am like her. In the last two years I, too, have learnt to distrust everybody, to expect to hear lies rather than the truth.

"Well," she says, stretching out her legs into my

space, "when they come, tell me. Then I might move." Her legs are wrapped in blood-stained strips of cloth. She continues to talk to her friend in the accent of a well-educated, rich woman. She begins to pick at the stinking bandages to get at the ulcers which ooze beneath. I try to turn away but I can still smell her.

I fold my arms upon my bended knees and rest my head upon my arms. I shut my eyes. I have discovered long ago that one rarely sheds tears when one cries during sleep. Yet I am so exhausted that I cannot sleep. Nor can I stay awake. I drift between the two. I have no idea of where we are and I do not bother to look out of the window. Those around me are secretively putting crusts of bread into their mouths and are taking sips of water from bottles and tins. I have nothing to eat but I feel neither hunger nor thirst. My excitement has vanished like late snow in the spring and shame squats like a rat on my shoulders and it gnaws at my brain.

I have only one thought in my mind: I should have gone back. I should never have got on the train. At the very least, I should have leapt from it as it drew away. I should have stayed with them.'

'But that wasn't the last train, was it?' I asked.

'No, there were other trains. People in the wagon were already talking about such things. And I was not the only person to have left someone behind. Nor would any of them have judged me. Those were desperate times, but it was no good. No comforting thought found space in my heart. I should never have left them. I had bought my freedom at the cost of theirs.

Then, one morning, though I am still in my corner of the train, I sense that something is different. I am not so alone, but I do not understand what has changed. Then I realise that during the night someone has put this rug around my shoulders. I discover that it was the old man from the logging camps, though probably, he was not nearly as old as I am now. He tells me that with his useless hands, he can never join the army now, but that I can, if I look after myself. The rug, he told me, was made of camel hair. It had kept him alive in Siberia, and now it could save me too. I did not tell him that I was hardly worth saving, because of what had happened, and he did not ask. I kept the rug around me and it was as comforting as the arm of a friend. Now it is threadbare in several places. Then it was thick and warm.'

'It's still nice,' I said and reached over to touch it. 'I thought it was a bearskin when you first showed it to me.'

'An easy enough mistake,' he smiled, 'for one who has not stroked a real bear. No, this rug is from the skin of a camel. I do not know where it came from, but the man who left it to the logger was a prisoner from the eastern regions of Russia, close to the Chinese border. It was not just Poles who suffered in those camps.

Now, the rug rested closely around me as the train made its way to the port of Krasnovodsk on the Caspian Sea. It kept me safe, like a wise and understanding friend, for I, who was so desperate to leave my childhood behind, was now as feeble as a baby.

I remember almost nothing else of that journey. I suppose a few people gave me bits and pieces to eat and drink. I'm certain that the man from the camps did, but when the train finally stopped at the station and we clambered stiffly down, everybody else seemed to have somewhere to go and someone to see except me. They had advised me to go straight to the officials from the Polish Army and to register. They would look after me, they would know how to help. I promised that I would. I even saw that man, the logger, waiting for me. And I went the other way.

Everyone was crowding around, getting news of when the next ship would come to carry them across the Caspian Sea and away from Russia, but I hung back. It seemed very bright and hot, though it was only the normal sunshine of a midwinter's day. I stayed in the shadow of a tall building and looked around cautiously. Suppose they asked me about my family? What could I say if I met someone I had known in Lvov? I might even meet my brother, Edward. I tried to imagine how it might feel if we saw each other across a street. How could I ever tell him what had happened to my mother and Josef?

Step by step I left the crowds behind me and slunk away. I followed the line of the shore. That first night I crawled under an upturned boat, wrapped the rug around me and fell asleep on the shingle. The next day I found my way back to the railway station and began to watch for their arrival from a safe distance. When darkness fell, I made my way back to the boat. Then, I have some luck: someone has left a small shopping bag down near the water's edge. I glance around. There are a few people about, but none are near. Casually, I wander over to it. I throw some stones into the water, which is oily and covered with scum. Nobody turns in my direction. I grab the bag, stuff it under the rug and keep walking. It is over in a second. I climb back up the shingle to the boat. Now my steps seem extraordinarily awkward and noisy. The soles of my boots flap and I stumble. Any moment someone will notice and cry out. Everybody will run in my direction. They will chase me and corner me and knock me to the ground. But it doesn't happen. I duck beneath the boat and lie there with the bag pressed to my chest, like a cat with its prey.

Still no one comes. I doze, for I'm faint with hunger. Sometimes I think I hear the silky lap of water on the stones. Then I hear voices. Someone is coming across the shingle. They slide and curse and lose their footing in the dark. They are not alone. A child replies. It speaks shrilly, swallowing back its tears. They go on again, then return. They are criss-crossing the beach. The man shouts at the child and swears and the child sobs its replies. I shudder. I know what they are looking for.

My heart pounds and pounds, but I never think to go and give it back to them. I feel around in the darkness above and find that I can wedge the bag up inside the boat. Only when their steps have finally faded do I manage to sleep.'

'Didn't you open it, then?' I asked.

'No. Not until the morning. I was more interested in hanging on to it, in outwitting them. I never thought that they might have thanked me, felt sorry for me, helped me even. Oh no. I did not care that they were poor people in trouble too. Suddenly, they were my enemies.

Everybody was my enemy now. It was as though I had reached the shores of another land, where hate and betrayal and shame must be my only companions.'

'But what was in the bag?' I had never heard anyone speak about themselves like that and it frightened me. I wanted to return to things which I understood.

'In that bag? Oh, it was food. Some cheese, some flour and a string of sweet, dried berries, threaded like a necklace. I imagine that the child had put down its shopping for a moment while it played along the shore, and then had run home, forgetting. For me it was good fortune and I never gave a thought to that child, who probably got a beating.

I spend many days watching for my family at the station, and returning to the boat at night. I am cunning. I always go by a different route, in case the authorities are watching out for me. I find one of the market-places and there, little by little, I exchange the rest of the tea for food and drink. My biggest problem is water, but it is winter and soon I'm drinking from the puddles with the dogs. Then, one night, I have my first taste of vodka.

I'm woken by the sound of fire. Instantly I'm alert. There is a smell of woodsmoke, the crackle of flames amongst old sticks and the sudden hiss of steam. I know what it is: it is a sound from my childhood, which is a thousand years away. It is the sound of an open fire blazing up under the stars. And I can smell food. I'm lured out, like a rat from its hole, and I see the stream of sparks gusting up into the sky.

The fire is down near the water and I think I can see several people sitting around it. I edge towards them. A couple of them have seen me, but they do not say anything. I take a few more steps. I can smell fish. The saliva pours into my mouth. I have not tasted fish for years and now I can hear its fat spattering down on to the embers. I creep closer. Their faces are red in the firelight. One of them looks at me again, a long, challenging look. I squat down. I can feel the warmth.

The one who had stared at me opened his mouth and licked his lips very slowly, watching me all the time. I've never seen such a cavern of a mouth. Then I realise that he has no teeth, only a few blackened stumps. One of them turns the spit and a rush of flames leaps up. In that light I notice that he has no shoes at all, his feet are not even bound in rags. They are black and thick with dirt. Another's flesh shines palely through the tears in his jacket. I do not understand what they are saying. It is not like any schoolboy Russian that I have ever spoken. Then the one without teeth speaks to me. It is a woman's voice. I'm horrified and perplexed. She speaks again, more loudly, and they all turn and look at me. She holds a bottle out to me and I reach to take it. Then she snatches it back and I fall forward with my face in the sand and stones. They laugh. I laugh too. She drinks again and offers it to me and I crawl towards her, still laughing. They move aside and I crawl on towards the fire and would have snatched the fish from the flames, if they had not held me back.'

'Were they drinking vodka?' I asked.

'Something like it,' he said. 'They were all destitute, desperate drunks, who would have tipped anything down their throats. But that night they made a place for me around their fire and they shared the bones and the skin of the fish and their vodka, or whatever it was. And I felt at home with them, especially after the bottle had gone round a couple of times. They were my people now.

I woke later to find myself still sprawled on the shingle, but now in the glaring light of day. I had the most terrible hangover that I can ever remember. I sat up unsteadily and discovered that I was not alone. The woman without teeth was sitting nearby, watching me. She gave me some water to drink and then made me a proposition. It took her some time to explain and even more for me to understand, but in the end I did. She would take me into her home and protect me, if I would work for her.'

'What did she want you to do?'

'To sell things. She made a sort of biscuit, just flour mixed with water and fried in a little fat over a fire, so I discovered. It was, of course, illegal for anyone to do any private business like that, that is why she wanted me to take the risk of selling these things on the street for her.'

'Did you do it?' It was hard to imagine, when I looked at Mr Wassilewska's neatly parted white hair and his well-polished shoes.

'Oh yes, I did it. I took my rug and my rucksack and the shopping bag from their hiding-place in the boat and followed her to her home.

I've never seen such squalor, not even in Kazakhstan. But she gave me a place to sleep in, under a table, and at least it was dry. I lived there for about a month.

Sometimes I collected driftwood for the stove on which she baked these biscuits. Often she was too drunk to do anything at all. Out on the streets of Krasnovodsk, I learn to be very alert. I watch for the secret police all the time and am chased, but never caught. One afternoon I watch as a rusting hulk of a boat limps into the harbour. Soon it is filled with Polish refugees. They are packed so thickly that they can barely find space to sit down on the deck. I see families fighting to get aboard. They are sailing to their freedom and I could have gone with them. Now I do not care. At that time I think I was more than a little mad.

The woman comes and goes and whenever she has a few extra coins she is down on the beach, drinking. One day she doesn't return. She has always got the flour for the biscuits and I suspect that it is stolen. Now I have nothing to sell. I wander the streets and pick up a few scraps after the market is cleared. Then one day I notice that there are men standing around near her house. I walk on, because they have the look of the secret police. I stay in the quieter, poorer streets, where nobody gives me a second glance, or if they do, it is to step out of my way. The port is still thronged with refugees and I still hear Polish spoken all around me, but I never speak it.

Two or three days pass when I eat nothing, though I find some scraps of fat left on a wall. I chew them and enjoy the saltiness. Then I see a man painfully limping down the street on the other side. He has some bread under his arm. I follow him. He pauses for breath and I stop too. I can hear him wheezing and struggling for breath, but he limps on, unaware that as dusk falls, he has another shadow. There are not so many men on the streets of Krasnovodsk. More and more have been called into the army and thrown into the dreadful struggle against the Germans. I imagine that this man was a wounded soldier. I creep closer, he falters, but does not turn round, and I strike him with my fist across the back of his neck. He stumbles. I snatch up the fallen loaf and run. But he has got up and is following. Still, he is only a cripple. I jump over a low wall and crouch there. He won't find me. I begin to tear at the bread with my teeth, then I hear his uneven step coming after me. He is hurrying, dragging his bad leg behind him. I'm cramming the bread into my mouth, wasting crumbs, which fall to the ground. He stops. I can hear his wheezing breath on the other side of the wall. I will knock him down. I will not let myself be caught, not again.

He looks over the wall at me with gentle, horrified eyes and I cannot hit him. He frowns slightly and I see the pity and the fear, but it is not a fear *of* me. He is afraid *for* me and he holds up both his hands and makes that soothing movement that you make to calm a nervous dog, so that it will not leap at your throat.

'Keep it,' he says, and there is no anger in his voice. He has already turned away. I hear him limping away, dragging that crippled leg along, and only when he is out of sight do I realise that he has spoken to me in Polish.

It affects me very much. I had not understood quite what a loathsome and pitiable sight I was. I'm filthy and half naked, with the rug flapping around my shoulders. The lice drip from my hair in grey, tangled ropes of filth. I stink so badly that the dogs in the street sidle over and lick me eagerly. My lips are cracked and bleeding and sometimes I cannot see at all clearly.

In my determination to forget what has happened, I have almost forgotten who I am. And I do not even dream of them at night. Now, I only have one wish: that no one will recognise me either.

Then someone does.'

'Who?' I asked.

'Peter.'

'Peter from your school? Who went to the mines?'

'That's the one. And he doesn't recognise me, oh no. He recognises the boy-scout rucksack that I still have slung over my shoulder. Later he told me that at first he thought I was dead and that this creature in the streets must have stolen the rucksack from my body. Then he says my name. 'Stefan?' he says and I try to run off. I am so ashamed. But he does not let me go and he too has changed. He has seen things in the mines that he will never speak of.

He doesn't ask me any questions. He tells me that he is waiting for his father who is in hospital with typhus, here in Krasnovodsk. He is sharing a room with several other Polish people, all refugees from the settlements and the camps. He insists that I go with him. We walk slowly down the street, side by side, and I wonder if he also remembers the time when we walked to school together, side by side. And I wonder if I ever really was that boy, but I never mention it. In fact, at that time we never spoke of our homes. It was too painful.

The people he is staying with take me in and clean me up and they never say a word. And they saved my life. I am quite certain of that. They shared their food and their cramped room and they include me in their endless discussions about what the future will hold for us. They even persuade me to register with the Polish Army.

I told Peter that I had become separated from my mother and Josef in the crowds at the railway station in Uzbekistan. He believes me and anyway we do not want to speak of the past. All our talks are about becoming soldiers; we are very keen. For me, at least, it is the hope of a new life and a new beginning.

Peter's father is slowly recovering in hospital. When we visit him he urges us to leave on the next available ship. He will stay until he is stronger and he promises me that he will look out for my mother and Josef. He is hoping for news of his brother who vanished in the deportations. He is very insistent. Though his voice is still gentle and kind, his eyes shift anxiously and he looks at least sixty years old. Peter does not want to travel on alone, but he cannot refuse his father.

And that is how I finally leave that desperate shore. With thousands of others we scramble aboard another old vessel, more sieve than ship, we joke. I have never been on the sea before and I now discover that I'm not a good sailor. I stagger across the swaying deck and throw up over the rails, and, I'm afraid, over some passengers too. I watch the lights along the shore grow dimmer and dimmer and finally fade and with a terrible, guilty joy, I realise that I have escaped, after all.'

9

Voytek

'WE ARRIVED IN PAHLEHVI, ON THE PERSIAN SIDE OF the Caspian Sea, in the spring of 1942,' Mr Wassilewska continued. He barely paused for breath; it was as if he was eager to reach another part of the story. 'And it was there that Peter and I finally joined up. I lie about my age, naturally. Then, there I am: a soldier in the Polish Army. A man amongst men, at last. More truthfully, I'm one more skeleton in uniform, amongst thousands of others. We are a sorry sight. Not only are we hungry and weak, but now malaria and typhus are raging through the army camps. It was very sad that so many men, who had survived so much, now died of these illnesses, there in the desert.

In that respect, I'm lucky. I do not fall ill. After several months of army food and training, it even looks as though one day I might fill out enough to fit the enormous uniform that has been issued to me. But I'm young and when I glance in a mirror, I smile and think that I make quite a handsome soldier! I enjoy army life. We are kept busy most of the time and I don't mind. It stops me thinking.

And soon I am in love again. Not for me a faithless Kazakh girl who scorns me and marries another. This time I have chosen a bear and, before you laugh any more, let me tell you that I am not alone! It is a very popular choice. Everybody is in love with this bear.'

'Is this "Voytek", the bear in the photo?' I asked.

'Yes. That's the one, and somewhere I have a little model of him too, though I can't remember where it is at the moment.'

'So where did this Voytek come from?'

'That is what I wanted to tell you. From the Hamadan Mountains in northern Persia. I am in a convoy of army lorries which is crossing these mountains on the way south. It is already very hot and we have stopped for a rest and a smoke. We settle ourselves in the shade of some big rocks. We have opened a tin of meat. Somebody tells a typical soldier's story about a Russian woman who was supposed to cook cats: she made them into cat soup, and it was very delicious, he said. Our laughter dies on our lips, something has moved behind the rock. I glance around. It is a lonely place. We have also heard of bandits. We hear another sound. Several men reach for their guns. A pebble is disturbed and rolls down. Some have jumped to their feet, others have taken cover. Then someone yells that it is nothing, just a kid.

I see a peasant boy in a dirty, knee-length robe. He stands barefooted amongst the sharp stones and he is holding something in a sack. He is about nine or ten years old and he is licking his lips. We relax and continue eating. He watches intently as we spear the meat from the tins and raise it to our mouths. I understand him. We all do. In the next moment we have smiled at him and he has smiled back. He wipes his hand over his mouth and pushes his hair from his eyes. Someone offers what is left in a tin and he looks at it with longing and with fear. The soldier encourages him and he drops the sack to the ground and begins to eat.

The sack moves. I notice it at once and nudge my neighbour. The boy has noticed it too, but he only grins

—— 99 ——

and chews rapidly. It is intensely hot and sometimes we hear rocks crack and fall into the canyon beyond. The sack stirs again, but the boy does not want to stop eating. We, however, are curious and persuade him to untie the neck.

Inside is a tiny bear cub. It looks at us, then up at the bright sun, then it sneezes loudly. It wrinkles up its button of a nose and sneezes again. It puts its front paws out of the sack and its claws are like two small black hands in the dust. It is as pretty as a toy and slowly we all gather round. The boy is excitedly telling us what has happened and though no one understands the language that he speaks, we can follow his actions. It seems that the mother bear had been killed by hunters in the mountains. This lad had picked up the cub after they had gone. One of the soldiers says that a bear like this can be trained to dance and do tricks. Gypsies took them round the villages and earned a living that way. We imagine that the boy will want to sell the cub.

I put out my hand slowly, but someone pulls it back, saying that bears are never tamed. This one will bite me with razor-sharp milk teeth. But it doesn't. It pushes its head against my hand and I feel its rough tongue on my fingers. I smile at the boy and he squats down near me. I stroke the cub's head and the boy grins again and pokes it with a stick. I do not think it was meant cruelly, but it looked cruel and a murmur of disapproval went round the crowd of soldiers. One of them picks the cub up cautiously. He holds it away from himself but it mews like a kitten and its back legs flail. When he leans against a rock, the bear settles down in his arms and its eyelids flicker.

We all fall in love. These hardened men, who have seen more types of death than you can imagine, are suddenly pushing each other aside as each tries to stroke the bear's head. We wonder how old it is and what type of bear it is. They begin to bargain and the boy, who is still squatting on the ground, squints up at them. They put some tins of meat and fruit into his sack and then some odds and ends from their pockets. The boy indicates that it is not enough. They begin to collect money. I contribute too. I want to help. I push through to get close to the little orphan and the soldier who was holding it puts it into my arms so that he can get out his wallet.

The creature trembles against me. I can see the dirt and dust engrained in its fur. I hold it closer and feel its heart beating against mine. I can smell its hot, animal smell. Its muzzle touches my wrist. I shiver, expecting it to bite me, but it doesn't. It shivers too and then, desperately, it begins to suck the side of my hand.

At last the boy seems to be satisfied, delighted even; he runs off over the hot stones with the sack swinging and bumping from his hand. The order comes for us to move off. We climb back into our lorries, swearing that we must keep the new member of our group a secret. I'm reluctant to hand the bear over, but the older men take him from me. They are eagerly telling tales of animals they had reared back home. They remembered lambs and calves and pups which had been abandoned or orphaned and which would not have survived if someone had not taken pity on them.

I recall our dog. The picture of her is unwanted and unexpected and I withdraw into the stuffy darkness at the back of the vehicle. I see her with her puppies in front of the blue, enamelled stove. When she had tired of feeding them she would stand up and shake herself but one or two would always cling on and she'd trot off with them still hanging there and we'd laugh uproariously. I do not want to remember anything else. The other men in the lorry are busy with the bear who is very young and clearly weakened from hunger. They have diluted some condensed milk with water and have put it in an old vodka bottle with a rug stuffed in the neck. The cub begins to suck and in a moment we all fall silent. Above the rumble of the lorry we can only just hear the eager panting sounds as it sucks and sucks. It is a small, private sound and it returns many of us to that world we have lost.

The bear, who has been named "Voytek", which means "little one", continues to thrive. The soldiers make a nest for him in a tin bowl, which they line with material, but it is clear that he much prefers to snuggle up in someone's arms. Whenever he can he climbs up on to a camp-bed at night, and settles himself against the warmth of the sleeper. Soon it is clear that he regards one soldier as his special guardian. They understand each other and it is clear also that Voytek is a special bear: he is unusually gentle and friendly. Everybody, as I told you, loved him and soon the secret is discovered. But there is no trouble: the soldiers get special permission for Voytek to remain with the company. He becomes a mascot, but for me, and for many others, he is much more.

He reminds me of all those things that I never speak of: of the safety and the warmth of home and family. I often think about the moment when the hunters entered the cave where he must have hidden with his mother. Did he understand? Had he been hurt and frightened, and had there been another cub or two that we didn't know of, hidden somewhere in the lonely blackness of the caves? Sometimes I woke suddenly in my tent at night and I didn't know if I had heard Voytek whimpering for his lost family, or if I had heard the wild animals of the desert howling at the high, bright moon. Or had I heard some other voice calling me from some other far distant shore?

So, we settled into our new training camp in the desert and now, whenever I was free of duties, I would find Voytek and play with him. I, who had been so scornful of childish things, suddenly longed to have my childhood back. I brought Voytek treats of chocolate and fruit and biscuits and he accepted them all and licked my fingers clean with his rough, red tongue. Secretly, I'm convinced that he likes me better than anyone else. When we wrestle – and we are all teaching him to wrestle – then, I bury my face in his thick, soft fur and for a moment, I'm back home in a world of warmth and comforting arms, where a hand will ruffle my hair and my little sister would sit on the end of my bed in the morning, in her new rabbit-skin cap . . .

When I am with Voytek I believe that I can reclaim my boyhood that was trampled beyond recognition on that long road from home. I can be a kinder, better person with this bear who loved me and would never know what I had done.'

Oh yes, we all loved Voytek. Men who had watched friends and brothers die in the frozen wastes of the north, now watched many others die of exhaustion and disease and they were helpless to prevent it. These men turned to this odd little bear cub for comfort and for entertainment. We played with him as you play with a toy. We swapped tales of the wicked things he had done, for he stole food and would go to any lengths to get hold of something sweet. One time I remember he tried to dress himself up in the underclothes belonging to the women soldiers and he ran through the tents with all sorts of frilly things stuck on his head and the girls ran after and we died of laughter. It was so wonderful to laugh.'

'In that photo, Mr Wassilewska, he looks enormous. He's bigger than you. When was that taken?'

'In Italy, I think. By then Voytek was fully grown and I remember that the Italians were terrified of him. And that would have been in about 1944. We stayed in the training camps in the desert for roughly two years and those were the years of Voytek's childhood. You could almost say that he and I grew up together, for I too changed a lot in those years.

'Now, shall I tell you more about those years in the desert, or shall I go straight on to Italy?'

'I'd like to hear about the desert, but can I ask you something first?'

'You can certainly ask. I do not know if I can answer.'

'Did Mum know this story?'

He looked at me very carefully. 'She knew some of this story, but not as much as I have told you.'

'But you said that she'd only been in your house once! How could she know?'

'Do you think that I lie?' It was the first time that I had seen him angry.

'No! I didn't mean that. I only wondered how much she knew . . . about . . .'

'About my losing my family?'

'Yes.'

'She knew about that. She asked if I missed them . . .'

'What did you say, Mr Wassilewska?'

'I told her about my mother. I told her what my mother had said to me, about the stars.'

'About still being able to look up and see them shine?'

He nodded.

'Why did you tell her that?'

'Because she asked me.'

It wasn't enough. It wasn't what I had hoped to hear, but then, I didn't know which questions to ask him. I got up restlessly. Suddenly, I didn't want to hear any more. I mumbled that I had to get back; that after all, the desert would have to wait until another day.

That night I heard the phone ring again. I was awake instantly. My heart pounded. I leapt out of bed and scrambled downstairs, but I couldn't hear it any longer. I stood in the darkness and waited. Maybe it would ring again. And why hadn't anyone else heard it? How could they fall into such deep and carefree sleep? Didn't they care as much as me? Then I saw the crack of light under

—— 104 ——

the living-room door . . . It was Dad. He was awake too, though really, it didn't look as though he'd been to sleep at all. Something flickered on the television, but he had turned the sound right down.

'I thought I heard the phone ring,' I said.

He shook his head but didn't look up.

'If it *had* rung, you'd have heard it, wouldn't you, Dad?'

'Probably.' He stared intently at the film. Then he offered me tea and when I'd fetched a mug, he poured me a cup which was stone cold. I drank it in silence.

'Do you think it was the phone?' I tried again.

He shrugged and switched channels.

'I've heard it before. Lots of times.' But he wouldn't listen to me. 'Mum was planning to leave us.'

'What?'

'She knew she was going to leave.'

'Don't talk such rubbish!'

'She did.'

'Go to bed, Richard. You really don't know anything about it.'

'I do.'

'What do you know?'

I wanted to tell him what Mr Wassilewska had said but I was afraid. Even if I had been able to explain it, would he have understood? And how much did I really understand? But I was certain, now, that she had been thinking of leaving us for some time. And she was afraid that she would miss us. That was why she had asked Mr Wassilewska about these things. Wasn't it?

I left Dad still sitting there. In my bedroom, I drew back the curtains as far as I could and I moved my bed so that whenever I opened my eyes I could look out at the quiet night sky.

10

A Change of Place

SOMEBODY HAD SEEN HER. THE PHONE STARTED ringing the next afternoon just before Auntie B and the others got back from another swimming trip. I didn't know what to do or say. Dad raced home from his office and spent ages with the police and Mum's agent. She'd been seen at the airport in Paris, in the departure lounge. An actor who'd worked with her a couple of years ago had called to say that he'd seen her. He was absolutely certain. They hadn't actually spoken because she didn't answer when he said 'hello', but he was still sure, he'd swear to it.

Dad was frantic. Benjy scowled in disbelief. That stupid actor, he said, was probably making it up.

'Don't you want her to come back?' I yelled.

'No,' he said and rushed upstairs. I followed and would have got him if he hadn't locked himself in the bathroom. I lay in wait outside.

Auntie B was frantic then.

'Why can't you just leave him alone?' she begged me. Her hair was still wet from swimming and her eyes were bloodshot.

'Why can't *you*!' I yelled back. 'He's not *your* child. Why can't you just leave us all alone!'

Dad was on the phone again, trying to buy an air ticket

to Paris. Tess stayed in the kitchen, silently making the tea. She'd bitten her nails down to the flesh and now they were bleeding.

I couldn't bear it any longer. I escaped and wriggled through the fence, although Tess was already calling that tea was ready.

In Mr Wassilewska's garden, yesterday's rain had made the roses glow. I'd never noticed how heavily scented they were. I broke one off, not realising what I'd done, then I glanced guiltily back at our house: this time I did not want anyone to see me.

He wasn't on the step and I didn't ring in case I made him angry again. I loitered by his pond where a pair of turquoise dragonflies darted and flickered above the still water like two well-rehearsed dancers.

Had Mum ever been to Paris? I realised that I didn't even know. In fact, I didn't know much about her at all. Strangely, I probably knew more about Mr Wassilewska's past than I knew about hers. And now? Was I never to know more? And was my small knowledge of her only to dwindle and fade and never ever be renewed?

The pointed attic windows of Mr Wassilewska's house were clearly reflected in the pond. Beneath them, darkly, some of the goldfish moved silently to and fro. I squatted down and watched. I could hardly believe that Benjy had actually stolen fish from here. Whatever had he done with them? Given them to his friend Jim? Fed them to the cat? I pulled some of the petals from the rose and let them tumble down on to the surface of the water. The fish swam up hopefully, their curious, pouting mouths moving in and out, and I was so engrossed in this that I didn't hear anything.

He pushed me from behind and I fell in with an almighty splash. It wasn't deep, of course, just muddy. I pitched into it head first and I suppose I must have looked ridiculous, when I stood up, with waterlilies and pond-weed draped over me. A couple of fish actually slithered off my T-shirt and fell back in. If it had been a scene in a film, then I guess I'd have had a fish-tail sticking out of my mouth too! Benjy was making his getaway through the currant bushes, but I didn't give chase. I was afraid that I might drag the rest of the pond life out with me. And anyway, what was the point? I wasn't so mad at him, after all, and what would I have said when I caught him? I didn't want another row, I just wanted to get cleaned up before anyone saw me, but I didn't even manage that.

Mr Wassilewska came back as I was rinsing my feet and trainers under his garden tap.

'I'm awfully sorry,' I began politely. I had intended to explain that it really hadn't been my fault, but when I heard myself, it didn't sound right. It had been my fault, in a way.

'Dear me.' Mr Wassilewska looked unhappily at the wrecked pond and then at me.

'I'll clear it up.'

'I should hope so! I don't like things to be messed up. Now, do you honestly want to hear about the desert or would you rather go and frighten my goldfish some more?'

'The desert, please. And the bear. And I am sorry.'

'Me too.' He nodded towards the currant bushes. 'Do you think he likes to hear as well?'

'Who? Benjy? No way! He doesn't understand things like that.'

'If you say so.'

'Anyway, he'll have gone home. He'll be with Auntie B.'

'Right. You want to change your clothes? No? Then don't sit too close. You smell as bad as that bear did.'

It took me a moment to realise that he was teasing me.

'That is what Voytek loved best,' he continued, 'he

loved to bathe, even in the mud. Of course he came from mountains where the caves were dark and cool and now, here he is, under that fierce desert sun, that touches everything. Poor Voytek, he gets hotter and hotter, so his best trick is to run away to the soldiers' showers and turn the water on! Then he lies down under the spray. He would stay there for ever, or until all the water in the camp is used up, if he is allowed to. And my, did that bear smell as he dried out! He smelt worse than the worst soldiers' socks.'

'So did you train in the desert, Mr Wassilewska, as a soldier?'

'Yes, I did. And I had chosen the transport division in the artillery corps. I learn to drive out there, and I like it very much. Other men are choosing things they think are more exciting: the infantry, the armoured division, the airforce even, but that is not for me. I am too restless, and my commanders, who are good men, they understand this. But as a driver, I am always on the move. I drive all over the Middle East, to all the places that you hear of now: to Baghdad in Iraq, to Jordan and Palestine, to Syria, to the great cities of Alexandria and Cairo. I saw the Pyramids and I swam in the Red Sea, and it was wonderful, truly wonderful.

Of course, I know that there is a war on, how can I ever forget? But, all the same, it was magical. When I was in Kazakhstan it was as dreary as a long, cold sleep. There was no colour, no music, and no laughter. As soon as I have escaped over the Caspian Sea it is different. I had noticed it first on the streets of Pahlevi when Peter and I joined up. All around there are people selling and people buying: there are stalls of fruit and sweetmeats, trays of cheap jewellery and bales of bright cloth; there are pies and postcards and guns and puppies and nuts and fancy silk slippers – I am amazed. Sometimes I wonder if I'm back in the old markets of Lvov: there is shouting and singing; radios play music from the back of dark, dusty shops and the call to prayer floats over us – five times a day. People sit in cafés and they drink mint tea and sherbet and crimson fruit juice. They eat ice-cream and pastries from pretty china plates. And they are laughing. I had forgotten that people did that.

Everywhere there are men, and women too, in uniform. Armies from many countries have their soldiers there. They remind me of migrating birds, resting up on the long journey to other, different climates.

I want to taste it and smell it all. I want to let the ice-cream melt in my throat and put my arms around the shoulders of the pretty girls who laugh in the streets. And I do. I must have colour and excitement, like a drunk must have his drink.

Others complain about life in camp, about the sandstorms and the flies and the unending white stare of the sun and about the dates to eat – every day, dates, bloody dates, they moan, but not me. It is not that I am braver or better than they, oh dear me no. It is just that I would rather be turning the steering wheel in the hot cab with the sand grinding between my teeth and the sweat pouring down my back than ever again be held in the grey grip of boredom.

I am a mad driver too, a real show-off. But, all the time I'm at the wheel, I'm watching the road. I'm watching the horizon. In the bustling bazaars and in the quiet, warm shade of an oasis, I'm looking for them. Perhaps they have come. Maybe I'll catch a glimpse of them. I scan the crowds who stand and gaze up at the slender, arrowed minarets of Baghdad. I watch the caravans of camels which cross the deserts on unseen paths. And I dream at night. Maybe I'll see his head of golden curls. Maybe I'll see her dark head, streaked with white. Maybe, amongst the khaki uniforms and veils and

—— 110 ——

Bedouin robes, I'll see her dress. Or hear his voice again, calling me.

For it is happening. Families are finding each other again. The Polish Army and the Red Cross are reuniting those who have not seen each other for two or three years. I have witnessed some of those meetings. At first they do not know whether to laugh or cry, but they do both, falling into each other's arms. Then they hurriedly push each other away as though they have been mistaken and have been in the arms of a stranger, and then they are crying again, and holding each other tightly.

Peter has been reunited with his father, who had waited on in Kvasnovodsk for that winter, but had heard nothing of my mother and Josef. In the end, he could wait no longer. He was sorry. "Maybe they went back to the settlement," I suggested, "to see if Edward was there." "Maybe," he said and smiled, but neither of us believed that they would have done that.

Still, I was happy for those who were reunited. I used to wander down to Voytek, to tell him about such things. He dozed in the shade of a palm while I told him of Peter's luck, and he understood. And was pleased for Peter. Honestly.

And tomorrow, I tell myself, who knows what tomorrow will bring? Soon I will be taking supplies right up to Alexandria in Egypt. It's a long drive, but I've volunteered. I like to keep moving. And I might see something along the way.

Then I hear that someone is looking for me. I do not leave my tent at first. I am so full of fear and hope that I cannot do anything. I am not very polite to this man who has come specially to find me, but he is not offended. He has heard that my name is Wassilewska. He was with another Wassilewska in the labour camp in Siberia, and, yes, it was an Edward Wassilewska. Now my heart beats again. We compare notes: an Edward Wassilewska from

—— 111 ——

Lvov – there is no doubt. This man and my brother were both captured by the Russians and they were good friends. They had worked with others as slave labour, building a railway line in Siberia. He tells me great tales of how they sabotaged the construction. In winter they packed huge slabs of ice under the railway sleepers. Then, in the thaw, the ice melted and of course the railway track that had been laid above it collapsed. Oh yes, he told me lots of exciting stories. Then, they had been separated, and my brother had been sent further south to work in the swamps. Now this man had heard that Edward was here, in a hospital in Alexandria, recovering from the malaria he had caught in the swamplands.

I am wild with excitement. I apply for leave to search for Edward when I am next in Alexandria. I half hope that he will not recognise me and I shave off my seven whiskers with such enthusiasm that I cut my face to bits! After all, I was a schoolboy then. Now, I am a soldier.

The military hospital overlooks the Nile and a nurse takes me up the echoing stone stairs. She is a red-haired Polish girl, and her white apron is like a great white sail. The ward is quiet. A long row of army beds stretches down on either side and a fans turns round and round in the warm, white air. It smells of things and I'm overcome by fear. Maybe it is *not* my brother at all, but somebody else's . . .

She points and I grip my cap between my wet hands and my boots squeak, and I look at the long lines of sick men and wonder what it was like amongst the swamplands.

"Stefan!" He shouts my name, and all the men look at me and him, and I must turn back, for I have passed him by and not recognised him. "Stefan!" he repeats and then explains to them all, "It's my brother, my baby brother!"

He has been very ill, but is getting better now, he

assures me, though he looks frail and thin. He cries as we talk, and I do not like that at all. Nor do I like the news that has reached him from Lvov: Stanislawa and Maria were arrested by the Germans. Stanislawa had been working for the Polish Resistance and Maria was with her the afternoon that the Germans stopped her in the street. They were both held in prison, but after two weeks Maria came home to our grandmother on the farm. Edward says that she is still there, but that she does not speak of what happened. In fact, Grandmother has written that Maria does not speak much at all and now is not like other little girls of seven. Stanislawa was taken east, into Germany, and there is no news of her. The Red Cross have looked on all their lists, and they have not found her name.

I cannot think about it. I cannot think about Stanislawa at all, because she was a girl who was always laughing. Even at her wedding, she had laughed, had bitten her lip to try and stop herself, but had set me off laughing too, and at such a serious moment: I had watched her in her wedding dress shaking with helpless laughter. Now, I laughed hysterically, for no reason at all.

High above me the fan spun and spun and moved the air in warm waves and I watched it. Then I looked out of the windows to where the sun was bright and the shadows were black. I wanted to escape. I could not bear to linger on amongst these raw, unhealed memories. I wished that I had not come.

"I'm glad Mother doesn't have to know," I blurt out, like the fool I am.

Edward looks at me. "Don't worry. I'll tell her," he says.

Now he has me trapped. He has already asked me about Mother and Josef an I have not answered him. I rushed straight on to other things. Now, of course, he asks me again. I try to explain that I do not know where they are. But how can I ever explain that I abandoned them?'

He shook his head unhappily and ran his hands through his thick white hair.

'But you didn't, Mr Wassilewska. You couldn't help it!' I said quickly.

'Couldn't I?'

'No. And you did it for the best, didn't you? You had to keep that space in the train free for them, didn't you? Especially for Josef, who was ill – you were trying to help, weren't you?'

'Was I? Are you sure?'

I shivered in my wet clothes. He got up and handed the rug to me and I wrapped it around myself gratefully.

'What did you tell your brother?'

'I told Edward exactly what you have told me. That I did it for the best, that I had to keep that space open. That I couldn't help it. I did not tell him that when my mother went back to help Josef, I stayed where I was . . .'

'You mustn't feel guilty. You didn't have time to go back.'

'Didn't I?'

I was freezing, despite the blanket.

'What did your brother say?'

'Again, he said what you have said. He put a hand on my arm and said, "You mustn't feel guilty."'

'So he wasn't angry?'

'No. If anyone could understand, it was people like Edward and the other men in that ward, but I did not know that then. Then, I only wanted to get away.

Before I could do that he and the other men begun to discuss the rumours which have been on everybody's lips. Now I learn more about "Katyn". Do you know about Katyn?' he asked.

'I've heard the name,' I mumbled from under the rug, 'but I'm not sure why.'

'Do you remember that when I was still with my mother in Lvov, we had had one letter from my father? It

—— 114 ——

was written when he was a prisoner of war in the camp, and he had asked my mother for some boots. You remember? After that, there was a silence. We received no more letters from him. Even in Kazakhastan, when we did get a few letters and parcels, we got no news and no letter from my father. And it is not just my father who is silent: now, all the Polish people are whispering the same rumour. Now these men were saying it aloud: thousands of Polish officers captured by the Russians at the beginning of the war in 1939 had been secretly shot. They had been taken out into the forests and shot in the back of the head and buried in huge graves. And the place where they did this terrible thing is called Katyn. It was just like what we hear may have happened in the war in the old Yugoslavia, in Srebrenica. There, thousands of men were taken away and shot, we hear.

Back then, in that hospital ward in 1943, I hear from my brother about Katyn. It is almost certain that our father was one of those officers who was killed at Katyn, by the Russians.'

'So it was true?'

'Certainly it was true. My father had been shot in 1940. Even before we left Lvov, he was dead. I'm convinced now that my mother, who loved him very much, already knew of this. She had "felt" it, in the way that you do, of people you love very much. And that was why she could be so strong and so determined when the Russians came for us. She knew that there was no one but her to save us. I thought that she was hard and cold and unfeeling, and especially that she did not love me. But I was wrong. If she had not been so hard, we three would never have survived on the steppe.

But I did not understand that back then. Then, I wished that my brother Edward would stop talking and that I could walk briskly away and be back on the desert roads. Then I would not have time to think and suffer. I would be safe in my little home in the cab of my lorry, with the smell of oil and petrol and with the windscreen wipers smacking to and fro across the screen, clearing a space amidst the black tide of flies and sand. I'd put my foot down on the accelerator and hear the sand whistle off the wheels and I'd be in another, better world.

And then, too, I was in love again! Not with a Jana or with a bear, well, not only with a bear, to be honest. This time I was in love with a girl of my own age. And for this, I have to thank Voytek too. One day I hear a great noise, a shrieking noise, but with giggling too, so I know at once that that's a girl's noise. You know what I mean?'

I nodded. I did, absolutely. It must have been the sort of noise that the girls on the top of the bus made. It terrified me.

'Now, if you expect that I rush out of my tent like a hero, you will be disappointed. I do look out, but I peep cautiously through the flaps. And I see this tiny little girl in this huge army uniform. She is holding something high up above her head and trying to get away from Voytek who is nudging her with his nose. She is so thin that her army skirt looks as though it will fall off her. Two other girls are watching at a safe distance and they are doing the shrieking. They imagine that Voytek wants to eat their companion. My girl is giggling more than screaming and though it is true that Voytek is dribbling with hunger, it is not a skinny little Polish girl that he fancies, it is the tinned fruit that she is holding up.

Oh dear me, she was such a thin little thing, arms and legs like matchsticks and all lost inside this army uniform that is several sizes too big for her. But she has such a beautiful smile – a dark-haired girl with this beautiful smile, that falls upon me like rain on the parched land. No wonder the bear likes her! I like her. I love her. Instantly. I am in love. You remember that proverb: "The best pears are eaten by bears"? It is on that occasion that I hear it. A friend has also come out of his tent and is watching the scene. He taps me on the shoulder and grins and says, "The best pears are eaten by bears!"

Yes. I fell in love with her, like you fell in the pond – splash! I cannot resist – I do not even try to. I tell everyone I meet. I have her photo always by me. The whole camp knows. Stefan, the mad driver, is in love.

And she loves me too! Happiness is mine and I cannot believe it. I think, "How can this be? In the middle of so much unhappiness, how dare I, how can I, be happy?"

I buy her, I remember, a small ring with a blue stone in it. The man who sells it to me tells me that it is a turquoise and that it is lucky. Even that ring is too big for her finger, so she must wear it around her neck on a gold chain. She has a brother in the army too. We three become good friends. After the war, we say, when we'll be quite old – eighteen or nineteen at least – then she and I will marry and will start a furniture business together back in Poland. It was her brother's trade, and her father's, and I am good with my hands, and after this wretched war is over, people will want lots of new furniture in Poland . . . Such a beautiful girl she was, Richard. Just like—'

'Like my mother! She was like my mother, wasn't she, Mr Wassilewska? Just like my mother!'

'Yes. She was exactly like your mother. The same beautiful eyes, the same smile. I thought I was dreaming when I first saw your mother. Some people believe that each of us has a double, somewhere in the world. Now, by some strange chance, the double of the girl I loved had come with her own young family to live in the house beside mine. I couldn't quite believe it.'

'Did Mum know? I mean, did she know that she looked like the girl you were going to marry?'

'Oh yes! I tell her straight away! I can't help it. I look over the garden fence one evening because I think I hear a child crying and there is your mother, so close, with your baby sister in her arms, and I know I am staring at her too much. So I try and explain.'

'But she didn't understand you, did she? There was a misunderstanding.'

I pushed the rug down. I wasn't feeling so cold any more.

'Perhaps there was,' he said quietly.

'There was. Really there was, Mr Wassilewska, she thought that you had been asking her . . . ?'

I couldn't say it. Suddenly, on the very edge of getting it all sorted out, I didn't know what to say to him. I didn't know what to ask. I was no longer sure what they had said to each other on that hot summer evening so long ago, when I had been asleep in my little blue bed, and when the pointed stars had still shone brightly.

'About that bear,' I said at last, putting the edge of the rug back up to my chin, 'about Voytek: he must have been really nice.' I wanted to return to the safer territory of the desert.

'Oh yes,' Mr Wassilewska smiled. 'He was. Always, I could go back to him and he would make me smile again.'

'Wouldn't you like something like that now? A pet or something? A kitten? Lots of old people have pets.'

'But I do. I have my old friend: my rug. I sit out here on the step, with my rug on my knee, and I think of this and that—'

'I've seen you. I saw you last winter. Even in the snow, I saw you! Though I don't suppose you ever saw me!'

'Never!' he exclaimed. Then I noticed that he was laughing at me. And pointing.

Something was moving up in the apple tree over the fence.

'It can't be,' I protested.

'It is,' he laughed.

And it was. Benjy's curious face emerged briefly, then retreated to the green safety of the frail branches.

11

In the Shadow of Monte Cassino

*B*ENJY HAD GONE QUIET. BOTH DAD AND AUNTIE B WERE worried about him. I was too, in a way. He seemed to be avoiding me so I guessed that he was still feeling bad about the pond thing. I'd forgotten it – well, almost. And that wasn't really true either: it wasn't that I'd forgotten, it was just that that fight didn't seem interesting any more. But Benjy was still too quiet.

The summer days limped along. Dad talked about a holiday. 'We must do something,' he said at regular intervals, but we didn't. He had flown to Paris to follow up the lead, but had found no trace of Mum. I suppose that might have disappointed Benjy, although he always insisted that he didn't care. It disappointed me a lot, even though I hadn't really expected Dad to find anything. I still got up very early so that I could be the first to catch the morning's post tumbling through the letter-box, but my heart didn't race in the way it used to. If I only knew where she was, at least that would have been better. She didn't have to come back, not straight away, anyway.

And to make things even worse, Mr Wassilewska had gone away too. He'd gone to visit an old friend who wasn't so well, but he had promised to tell me about the Italian campaign as soon as he got back. I really missed him.

Auntie B said that I mustn't overstay my welcome, but I didn't listen. I mean, who was she to talk? I gave him half an hour after I saw the lights go on in his house and then I was over there, tapping on the window.

I think I startled him, but he came to the door with a big smile on his face and his arms outstretched. I'm sure that he was pleased to see me. He had, he said, some more poppyseed cake, a whole one, this time. His friend's wife was an excellent cook. He made coffee and cut two large slices and I carried the tray out on to the step. Guiltily, I noticed that his suitcase was still standing in the hall.

'So you know Italy, a little,' he remarked. I nodded, my mouth full of cake.

'When I went there in 1944,' he said, 'I thought that I did. I had never been before, but it was not a strange and distant land. Maybe it was because we were Catholics, and Italy, of course, is the home of the Pope, but we had always felt an attachment to that country. Nobody in my family had travelled there, but many in our town had. I had seen their crosses, their pictures of the Virgin Mary, their bottles of Holy Water, and I'd listened to their traveller's tales. My history teacher in school had been and had told us a lot about the beautiful cities, the Roman theatres and the famous artists and sculptors. Now, when the corps hears that we are going to Italy to fight, we are all very excited. For me, it feels like the first step on the road home.

For about two years we have been in the army, waiting and training, waiting and regaining our health and strength. When I see my reflection I am amazed: that miserable, skinny schoolboy is now a real soldier. I have been equipped and armed. I have done exercises in the mountains in Iraq and I have fired guns in the deserts of Syria. I am a soldier, but a soldier in waiting. I have not yet seen the face of my enemy. I have not even heard the sound of his guns. Now, at last, I will.

Our orders are to return to Alexandria. From there we will sail to Italy. "Action at last," I whisper to Voytek, because everybody knows that although Italy has surrendered, the Germans are still defending their positions there, in the north. "When I see the enemy, I will spit on him and stamp his ugly face into the ground!" I promise Voytek. Oh yes, I am such a brave young man. But can you guess what I really do, the evening before we leave?'

'Get drunk?' I suggested.

'Maybe, but that I cannot remember. What I can remember is creeping down through the tents to say goodbye to Voytek. It is a clear, clear evening and very cold. It is February and the desert nights are bitter at that time.I have some chocolate and some beer. Both are his favourites. We will share them. I stroke his head and he rolls over like a great big dog. He wants me to scratch his stomach, and as I do he waves his paws about like a puppy. His claws are long and black. He could have cut my flesh to ribbons with one blow, but I know that he won't. It is wonderful to trust a creature like that, but I'm glad that nobody much is about because suddenly I am crying. They are real tears and I wish that the stars did not shine so brightly and that the night was dark and cloudy. I'm afraid that my heart will break: and I do not want anybody to see. I'm not crying because I'm afraid. Oh no. Not me! Nor because this terrible war has torn apart everything that I loved. Never! Not even because I have already said goodbye to the girl I love. Of course not! I'm a soldier, aren't I? Soldiers put aside things like that, don't they? Anyway, that's what I've always been told. So, I'm only left with that bear. I cry about that. I do not want to say goodbye to him. That's all. That's all I cry about.

Then I discover that I'm not the only one. I hear

footsteps and another soldier appears. He too has come to say goodbye. Then another. We are all anxious and upset. What will happen to this creature who has lived with us for two years? He is our baby. He has grown up with some of us younger men, and has certainly learnt his good manners from some of the older men. He needs us, we say, and must not be left behind. But of course, on the eve of battle, it is we who need him.

Well, for the moment we are saved from worry. The Polish officers at the port get special permission for Voytek to embark on the ship, as a member of the company. He will not be left behind. And he's not alone. Imagine it! The quayside thronging with soldiers and officers and kit and supplies, trucks and all the usual crowds of local people, and in the midst of this chaos a great cheer goes up: Voytek is marching smartly up the gangplank followed by a dog, a monkey, some little animals in a cage and a parrot, I think! They are all pets of the soldiers! All have been given official permission to embark. People who do not know about Voytek think they have drunk too much the night before and are seeing things. But they weren't. Those animals did board the ship. Then, the huge anchor is drawn up and the engines are already throbbing deep down in the engine-room. The fleet turns slowly, and heads out of port and into the sparkling blue seas. And I am on my way again, only this time, I have chosen to make the journey. It is as though Poland itself lies just across this sea. This time I am not going to Asia or Africa. This time I am going home to Europe. Soon it will be spring. In the forests of my home the thaw will come and the snow will slip from the branches, and soon, soon, I tell myself, I will be home.

We landed at Taranto in Italy and I certainly was relieved. Midway across it blew up rough and I was so very sea-sick. So was Voytek. He has been on deck in a big crate by the mast, and has been very miserable. But he and I recover on dry land. And what a land: spring is already here in the Italian valleys, although I see snow on the distant mountain-tops.

It is so beautiful – almost as beautiful as Poland, although I would never have said so. The almond and apricot trees soon bloom and in little white villages on the hillsides people are beginning to recover from German occupation. We are near enough to the beach to go swimming and sometimes we take Voytek with us. He and I swim in the Mediterranean for the first time. Women and old men are working in the vineyards again, and children wave as we pass by. The air smells of sunny hilltops and white clouds, and every day it gets warmer. I think that I'm in Paradise. But I am wrong. At the base camp I begin to meet old men of twenty and twenty-two, whose faces are lined and drawn, and whose eyes are tired. They have been fighting almost without a break since before the winter. Their tales are not of Paradise but of Hell, and the place where they encountered Hell, they say, was called Monte Cassino. You know about Monte Cassino?'

'Not really. Was it a mountain?' I thought I remembered that the Italian for mountain was 'monte'.

'Monte Cassino was an abbey, the largest and oldest medieval abbey in Europe, I believe, and yes, you are right: it was built on a mountain, above the town of Cassino. The Allied soldiers have already attacked it three times and three times they have been beaten down by the German defenders, with terrible losses. Monte Cassino, these exhausted men tell me, is an impossible place to capture.

It stands on top of steep, rocky cliffs and the Germans have dug themselves in all around. They can see anything that moves. The abbey has already been bombed and the roof has collapsed but the walls still stand. The ruins themselves are so massive that they are like further fortifications. Tanks can't get through, they say. The Germans left inside are better protected than before and they are experienced, brave fighters, from one of the crack divisions. One day I get talking to an American soldier who has a Polish mother, so we can speak Polish together. He tells me about the desperate winter attacks up the steep, snow-covered sides of the mountain, where there was no cover and where the Germans picked off his comrades one by one. Those that were left were so cold and exhausted that they could barely crawl back to safety. I listen to him in silence, but I comfort myself with the thought that I, Stefan, know everything about cold and hunger. I, maybe, would do better in battle than these men.

Then news races around the camp: there is to be a fourth assault and we Poles have been given the task of capturing Monte Cassino.

"At last," I say and clench my fists. I may still have not seen my enemy, but I've heard his guns now, and I'm already excited. But I'm occupied all the time now, as we prepare for the attack. I'm driving ammunition to near the front line, as are the men who look after Voytek. I see him regularly. He was so miserable when they left him alone at the base camp that in the end they took him along – and there he is actually unloading boxes of ammunition, just like the men, from the back of the lorry. Sometimes he climbs up a tree and peers across the battlefield like a lookout. Then our hearts are in our mouths – but luckily no one takes a pot-shot at him. I secretly envy him his good view: I've seen the explosions of the German guns and I've heard the sound of their shells coming over, but of their eyes and their expressions I still have no knowledge.

This final attack on Cassino, our attack, will start at 11.00 p.m. Now, the unusually good meal that they have given us turns in my stomach. The atmosphere has changed. Some men are crouched in corners quietly writing letters home. Others are hastily checking their equipment, avoiding each other's eyes. There is much coming and going and tempers are lost. Some men are wild and some, like me, are tortured by the grip of fear.

For, of course, fear was not a stranger to me: it had first rested its hand upon my arm on the night when they took us away. Oh yes, I thought I knew about fear.

That night my orders are to drive again. I'm relieved. Others dread the winding mountain road that is exposed to enemy fire in places, but I'm just thankful that I don't have to crouch somewhere in the darkness and wait. That is my nightmare.

At 11.00 p.m. exactly the bombardment begins. Our guns open up over the whole front line. I can't describe the noise: the ground and the air shake with sound. Even when I'm in the lorry it is like being in a tin that some monster shakes up and down so that we are beaten against the sides again and again. And that is it: that it goes on and on so . . .'

He fell silent, listening, I'm sure, to something that I couldn't understand and seeing things that he did not even want me to imagine.

'The next evening,' he continued, 'in the dusk, when we have been fighting all day, I finally see the face of the enemy. I've taken reinforcements up and am driving down with a couple of wounded men in the back and I see five or six more staggering down the road that has been destroyed at the edges and is slippery and treacherous. Two are limping, another is being dragged between comrades. I slow down. The men in the back shout to get a move on. The dragged man lifts and turns his head and the bandage slips down. He has no eye. His mouth is open and bloodstained. Perhaps he has spoken. His lips have moved but I have not understood, not even heard him. He's young, a red-haired boy, as young as me, and

—— 125 ——

his fluttering hand is as thin as mine. I see it suddenly, quite close to me. He has this silver ring on his finger and I think, "Someone has given him that." The men in the back curse. His companions step aside from him and for a moment he sways, then falls down in the road. My mate in the cab tells me not to waste my sympathy on German prisoners and only then do I realise that that is what they are. When I look in my mirror I see him still sprawled in the road. The guard has moved the others on. His hair is still as bright as a leaf or a scarf dropped in the muddy road along which a long line of vehicles is crawling. I put my foot down and swing the truck so sharply round the rocky bend that I feel the wheels skid and slide. But I don't care. I do not want to see the face of my enemy when I look back again.

We are still fighting a week later. At the end of it we have captured, and just about held, two of the hills but not the abbey of Monte Cassino. Not yet. So many men have been wounded and killed that reserves must be hurriedly brought up for the final assault. It is that moment in a battle when both sides are exhausted: but it is not an excess of courage that will decide the outcome, but a failure of will. Now, I'm told that I'm no longer to drive. I'm to be part of the reinforcements for the gunners. I'm taken up through the lines at night, under the cover of darkness. I do not ask what happened to the other man, but they show me where he had been. That is my place, for now, they say. One of them helps me dig the foxhole a bit deeper. Two of them are occupied siting the gun on the places across the valley where they think the German gun positions are hidden. It is a long, dark, moonless night. They have been here for several days. We can only whisper briefly and move with great care so as not to draw enemy fire. I am so near to the enemy that sometimes I think I hear them speak. I wonder if any of the other men can guess that this is what terrifies me most: to be ordered to stay and wait. But I cannot speak of it to those who have already endured this for days on end. We wait. Dawn breaks, and still we must wait.

The next attack is to be made in daylight, and as the night falls back I see that the ruins of the abbey are still crouched there, waiting for me. They are like some hideous, unfleshed skeleton that will not die. When the attack begins, it is as though it is coming back to life and the stones themselves are stirring and reaching out for us and our warm blood. And I'm sure that they will reach me, in the end, if I must stay there any longer.

When the order to advance comes, I'm glad, for I've not yet trodden a battlefield. In those seconds, when we are scrambling over the top, awkwardly taking the parts of the gun and the field telephone with us and hoping and praying that we will not be shot, suddenly I realise that I'm not sure what we are supposed to be doing. We don't know where the mines are. I'm about to wet myself, which I hadn't expected, I don't know what to do. Above all else, I don't want to be left behind. In that moment when I climbed over the top – and now I can't tell you if it was long or short – in that moment, I see the green pastures that lay below the forests of my home. It is a sunny day and the grass is knee high. We're rolling down the slope, going over and over and trying to get giddy, as carefree children do, and I can smell the extraordinarily sharp smell of flowers and herbs that are crushed under my cheeks . . .

And do you know, to this day, I'm not even sure if I really did see that, or if I only told myself later that that is what I saw as I started across the battlefield . . .'

'Why? Why would you do that?'

'Because,' he drew a deep breath, 'maybe because later, a very little later, when we are only yards from the gun emplacement, there was only me who was alive, and the blast of the landmine had knocked me to the ground like trampled corn.'

He shrugged and finished the rest of his cake. When he leant back and looked out over the mild summer valley, I wondered what he really saw on the green hillsides.

'Weren't you frightened?' I asked eventually. I knew it sounded stupid and ignorant, just to ask like that, but I needed to know.

'Frightened?' he echoed mildly. 'Oh yes, I was very, very frightened.'

'So, so what happened. I mean . . . if you were, well, all right . . .'

'Frightened,' he repeated as though he had not heard me. 'I don't think it is "fear" that is important. We are all "frightened", or ought to be.

I have met many cowards who say that they were not frightened, but I have never met a brave person who says that. We *should* be frightened, shouldn't we? Ought we not to fear things that can harm us, or people even, who can harm us? We must have fear in our hearts, but what we must also have is courage. At least a little bit of it, now and then. And most of us do, I think. The soldiers on that battlefield had courage, both we and our enemy: and my little brother did too.'

'Who? Josef? Really?'

'Oh yes. Though it took me many years to appreciate it.'

'Do you think my brother Benjy has it?'

It was also a stupid question. After all, how could Mr Wassilewska answer that? He hardly knew Benjy. I couldn't imagine why I'd asked him. I expect that I'd glanced up and seen the apple tree quiver and the question had just popped out.

'Certainly,' he said promptly. 'It takes courage to steal!'

I scowled. I definitely hadn't expected him to say that.

'But what do *you* think?' he asked.

'Me? I've no idea,' I said quickly. 'And anyway I'd much rather hear more about Italy. If that's all right.'

'Of course. Where was I?'

'You were alive . . .'

'That's right. I was alive. And so, it turned out, was somebody else. I made it into a bomb crater. That gives me some protection and I'm just digging in a bit and realising that I've no idea what to do next when I hear this noise. A sort of tap, tap, tap. I think: that's it, finally, for me. It's a German, creeping up to get me. It's what I've always dreaded: being imprisoned in some place and not being able to get away. I can definitely hear this tapping. I shut my eyes and I can still hear it – amongst all the noise of battle, I can hear it, faintly, only it doesn't get any nearer. I decide to make a run for it. I think I'll go forward. This isn't courage – oh no. Remember, I'm the man who cannot bear to be left behind, so do you think I'll run back? Not me! I will go forward to find others. I'll face anything rather than this.'

'Was it a German?'

'No. It is one of our men, the telephone operator. I almost step on him, as I dash for the next crater. He is tapping with one stone on another to attract attention. I can see that he is badly wounded – a real mess. He manages to whisper that I must take the field telephone from him, and if it is still working, report back on what is happening. He is right, of course. Battles are only won when men fight together: we can do little on our own. Poor communications and reconnaissance helped lose the earlier battles, they say.'

'Is that what you did, Mr Wassilewska?'

'Yes. I get this man into the crater too, and dig him in a bit and then we stay out there together.'

'What happened to him? Did you stay with him all the time?'

'No. It was not quite like that: he stayed with me. I got

—— 129 ——

the field telephone working and since I was pinned down, I discovered that I had a front-seat view of the battle. I was perfectly positioned to send back an account of what was happening and I was ordered to stay. Our task had been to take the abbey at any price, so I must try to pay. And that man, in all his agony, did not leave me alone until I told him that I'd seen the Polish flag go up over the abbey. Only then did he sigh and let himself die.'

'So you were sort of "there", in the middle of it with this man who was dying, but you didn't get hit?'

'Not on that day. Later, yes, in another battle in Italy near the River Po, but on that day all I had to do was stay there, and endure it, and not to move on. It was, for me, the longest and the worst of days. But do you know what helped us?'

I shook my head.

'In my pack, I have my old friend, the rug. I take it out, and wrap it around us both and I draw the edge right up to my chin and it shielded us. I'm convinced of that. Though you may laugh.'

'That's what you still do, isn't it?' I said.

He smiled at me and nodded.

'So was Monte Cassino captured?' I asked.

'Oh yes. Though the price was high. My brother paid with his life.'

'Edward?'

'Yes. And many, many other friends. But Peter survived.'

'Peter, who you met again in Krasnovodsk?'

'That's right. Peter, who is in Glasgow now. That's who I've been to see. He's not so well and we like to keep in touch: people like him are our families now. Now we are able to talk about the old days, back in Poland, when we were schoolboys. I've told him about you.'

'Really? What did you tell him?'

'That you were interested – that you were a good listener –'

'That's not much.'

'Not much!' he protested. 'Not much! You've no idea – I'm sorry. I shouldn't have shouted like that. It's just that usually people *aren't* very interested. I never forget one man I was talking to. He's asking me what I'm doing in England, and I'm trying to explain. I tell him about 1940, about the Russians coming in, and you know what he says? He says, "You shouldn't have let it happen. *We* wouldn't," he says, "*we* don't let people come into our houses at night. *We* don't let them take us away!" And this was a man who wouldn't say "boo" to a traffic warden. He was so boastful and so ignorant that I decide that I will *never* speak of those things again. It is too painful. To be misunderstood is worse than to be silent. And I haven't been able to speak of these things, not until you asked me. So don't ever tell me that being a good listener "isn't much". To me, it means a great deal that I can talk, for I'm not the person to write of this. I still hate to write.'

I was rather embarrassed and glad that he had to go into the house to get more coffee. It took some time, but I didn't mind because I needed time to think. When he came back I knew what I needed to ask.

'*When* did Mum ask you about the stars, Mr Wassilewska? And why did she want to know?'

12

The Cheering of Crowds

'THE "WHEN" IS EASY ENOUGH,' HE REPLIED. 'SHE asked me this spring.'

'But she never speaks to you! She was almost rude, wasn't she? Though I'm sure she never meant to be.' I felt guilty speaking about her like that. 'I mean, she never even said hello to you, did she? So, how could she have *asked* you?' My mind raced. I dreaded what I might hear.

'Your mother was in the garden when she asked me. She was planting something, I think, in the spring, when it was so mild.'

'She planted lots of new things this spring. Dad said that the garden had never looked nicer.'

'He was right. Well, that day, your mother walked over to the fence with the spade still in her hand, and she called to me . . .'

'But she wouldn't have! She said you were . . .' I could have bitten my tongue off, but he didn't seem to have noticed.

'She called me by name. "Mr Wassilewska!" she called, but very nervously, and I was already thinking that I must have done something else to upset my neighbours. 'Mr Wassilewska,' she repeated, 'do you never get homesick?'

'Homesick? Why would she ask you something like that?' But I already knew, almost.

'I, too, was astonished. I didn't know what to say, it was so unexpected. But, like I said, I could see that she was very nervous, and perhaps upset. And I was always sorry for her . . .'

'Sorry for Mum! Why?' I shouted. I was outraged. How could anyone be sorry for Mum? They should be sorry for me, but not for Mum. Never!

'I was sorry that she was not happy,' he said quietly.

As I heard his words I knew they were true. I held my breath and counted the railings around the steps. There seemed to be nineteen, which was an unlikely number, so I counted again and then made it twenty-three, which wasn't any better. For a moment I saw her face very clearly. She wasn't smiling. He was right. She had been unhappy. Had Benjy known? Or guessed? And Dad? Had I been the only one who hadn't noticed?

And so what?'

What did her happiness matter besides ours?

Didn't she care that Tess now bit her nails until they bled? And me? Had she ever cared about me?

I got up so that I could count the railings properly, touching each one, to be sure.

'There's twenty-one, and that one half round the corner,' he said. 'I didn't space them quite right!'

I shrugged. If it had been my house, I would have kicked them down, one by one, if I could.

'*Are* you homesick?' I said at last, not looking at him. 'Are you homesick, Mr Wassilewska?'

'Sometimes, yes. I suppose I am.'

'And what do you do then?'

He came over and leant on the railing beside me and pointed to the darkening sky above.

'You look up at the stars, don't you?' I said.

He nodded.

'And that's what you told Mum, isn't it? You said "yes, sometimes," so she asked you what you did to comfort

—— 133 ——

yourself and you told her that you looked up at the stars, just as your own mother had. That's right, isn't it, Mr Wassilewska?'

He nodded again.

'Yes,' he said, 'that's it exactly, word for word. Now, shall I get us more cake?'

I shook my head. He looked exhausted and I was, too. I apologised for having been in his way after the journey, but he only laughed and said, 'Any time'.

I went back through the fence and suspected that Benjy might still be up in the apple tree. When I walked underneath, I called out 'Night night, sleep tight.' After a moment, his hesitant reply rustled down from between the leaves, 'And think of me, when the mouses bite . . .'

It was what Mum used to say, sometimes.

After that it rained torrentially for about a week. It was as if someone had torn the end off the summer and let autumn flood in. Tess, being Tess, was busy getting ready for school: she liked to have every pencil nicely sharpened and every sock neatly named. I didn't bother. I intended to go over to Mr Wassilewska's, but it was raining too hard. Each time I thought about it and looked out of the window, I felt faint-hearted and turned away. I messed around at home instead. I was so bored that I even played Lego with Benjy. People say that rainy weather makes you tired too and I'm sure they're right: for the first time in ages I slept late and didn't even hear the post. Auntie B teased me and said that oversleeping was a sure sign of school approaching. She also told me, in confidence, that she hadn't enjoyed school that much either. I was quite surprised. I had always imagined that she was the kind of girl who'd been the eager prefect type. No way, she said, not when she was young.

'Did you know Mum when she was young?' I asked.

'Not really. Not when she was a schoolgirl, if that's what you mean. I didn't meet her until your father brought her into the office after they were engaged. I suppose she was twenty-three or twenty-four then, and that's still quite young.'

'Was she . . . the same?' I asked.

Auntie B stopped peeling potatoes and was staring at the rain.

'The same? What do you mean, Richard? Are you asking me if she was as beautiful?'

'No. I'm asking if she was unhappy back then?'

'I'm not sure,' she said. 'Why?'

'Mr Wassilewska said she was unhappy.'

'Did he?'

'Yes. But he didn't say why.'

'How strange.'

'Do you think I should go back and ask him?'

'Yes, I do.'

'But it's raining . . .' I muttered pathetically.

She pointed to the umbrella.

'Do you really think I should go?'

'Why not?'

'I don't know. I don't know what to talk about either.'

'What do you usually talk about?'

'Nothing much, though sometimes he tells me about this bear. It's called Voytek.'

'There you are then. Start off with that.' She came to the gate with me and watched as I splashed off through the puddles, and I was sorry that I wasn't nicer to her.

It took him ages to come to the door and the moment I saw him I knew that something was wrong.

'It's nothing,' he said when I asked. 'Just a touch of old age.'

He took me into the kitchen which was rather warm and asked if I minded staying in there today. He was feeling cold, he said. There was several days' washing-up in the sink and the normally bright room was dusty and dishevelled. While he was searching for clean coffee cups, he picked something off one of the carved shelves and held it out to me. It was a small, china model of a brown bear.

'Voytek?' I asked, taking it carefully from him.

He nodded.

'So Voytek really was famous?'

'Oh yes. And after Monte Cassino, which was such a great victory, he was even more famous. Everybody wanted to meet the bear who had fought at Monte Cassino. When I finally got back to base camp after my wound had healed, I almost had to wait in line to see Voytek!

I find he is the most popular soldier in the army and certainly the most handsome. He is magnificent: fully grown and about seven foot when he stands on his hind legs. He's quite a frightening sight, if you do not know him. Always he is a celebrity. The local farmers and village folk have got used to him now – they had to, for he has spent all summer gorging himself on their fruit. At first, though, they were very afraid. Now they are almost as fond of him as we are.

And Voytek has remained gentle, unusually gentle, I believe. There is only one thing he hates, and that is donkeys. Once, back in Egypt, when he was just a very little bear a donkey made that dreadful noise of theirs, just under his nose. "Braying" – that's what you call it, isn't it? It terrified him and he never forgot. Now, whenever he saw a donkey in Italy, or even a horse, he would try to run away and if he couldn't, he'd cover his eyes with his paws so that he wouldn't have to face that wicked, braying animal. Poor old Voytek.'

'Did the Italians make this little model of him?'

'No, no. That was made here, in England.'

'So even people here had heard about Voytek?'

'And not just heard! But do you still want to listen to all this?'

'Yes, I do. But not if you're too tired. Or anything,' I said, awkwardly.

'All right. But you stop me if I talk too much. I think that maybe I said too much last time.'

'Not at all. It was really interesting, about Italy and Monte Cassino. And there are things I want to ask.'

'Ask then.'

But I didn't ask. Not yet. Instead I said the first thing that came into my head.

'About Josef . . .' I began.

'What do you want to know?' he said sharply.

'Just whether, just if . . .' I was floundering, losing my footing amongst things that I didn't understand. 'Just if you heard anything, while you were in Italy. I mean, he'd have liked Voytek, wouldn't he? You could have told him all about Voytek, couldn't you . . . ?'

'Yes,' he said softly. 'I could have. And you are right, of course. Josef would have liked Voytek, very, very much. Especially that summer. When I had rested a bit and the wound was fully healed, and the fighting in Italy was nearly over, it was a good time and he would have enjoyed that – though of course the soldiers' families were not in Italy. They had been sent all over: some to India, some to East Africa – that's where Peter's father was sent. But all the same, Josef would have enjoyed that summer in Italy. He would have been thirteen? twelve? and he would have loved Voytek, who all this time is getting fatter and fatter. Sometimes he is lying down flat on his back under the vines and eating the grapes which dangle about him. We say he is like a Roman Emperor: too lazy to move. Often we take him to the sea and he is so excited then, splashing about and swimming like a child.

It is a strange time for me – for all of us. Suddenly, after so much action, so many changes, so many losses, we are left with nothing much to do. Certainly, we are busy: one always is "busy" in the army; I am back driving. I have a medal for bravery and I have been promoted too. So I am a little proud at this time. And, if I'm truthful, a lot drunk! The Italians may not have much else left, but they still have quite a lot of dreadful wine. The Germans have drunk all the decent stuff, before they retreated, we say. But I'm happy enough with what is left.

Yet we envy the Italians: the Germans have gone from their land, but not from ours, and news from Poland is not good. But, I am young, and the sun shines and I share a bottle now and then with Voytek and, like any young man in love, I'm waiting anxiously for letters from my fiancée who is with the Polish Army in North Africa.'

'Was she all right?'

'Yes, and her brother too. So I am very thankful, but not as thankful as I would like. In all her letters she writes eagerly of the plans we had made. As soon as this war ends, she wants to return to Poland. She must, she writes, go back and find out what has happened to the rest of her family. Of course, I understand. We must meet in Poland, she writes, when the war is over. Then we can marry.'

'Didn't you want to do that?'

'Of course I did. It is all that I dream of, to marry her. To have my own family. And I, too, think of my relatives: my sisters, my grandmother – our house. Our town. But I also know that Stalin's Russian Army has occupied Lvov. Indeed, great areas of Poland lie under their shadow and will stay there. The politicians have already made their secret agreements. If I go back, I will be putting myself under the same shadow. I do not know if I can endure that again. I beg her to think carefully, to wait. I remind her how difficult it was to leave Kazakhstan. If she goes back to Poland, I warn her, the Russians may never let her leave again.

And I'm not alone in my fears. For years we have all stayed alive in order that we might go home. Now it looks as though our country and our homes are no longer there and we must set out in another direction.'

'That's awful,' I protested.

'It was so very sad. It broke our hearts.'

'So what did you do?'

'For the moment, nothing – the next decision is made for me. My company is sailing for England, so that is where I must come.'

'And what about Voytek?'

'He comes too! He had his own place on deck again, and again he is our main entertainment – so long as the weather was good.

We fixed up a ring on deck and held wrestling matches with him: even against two and three men he can always win, if he wants. So, he wrestles and tries to catch seagulls and has a fine time until the sea gets rough. Then he lays down with his great head on his paws, and his eyes are half-closed and he groans. He is as sick as a sick cat. And me too. I'm a poor sailor. It is a long voyage, and when we see the docks in Glasgow, I don't know who is more pleased, Voytek or me.

And once we are ashore, on dry land, it is even better. Huge crowds come to welcome us – for people have heard of the bravery of the Polish Army. It makes us feel good. Now we march in columns, as smartly as we can, with our medals on our chests. Through the streets we march and the crowds are cheering, at least I think they are, because I couldn't understand a word – and who do you think is at the front?'

'Voytek?'

'Of course, marching like a professional. The crowds couldn't believe it. They go wild, cheering him loudest of all, and he loved it.'

'I'm glad they cheered,' I said.

'Me too,' he nodded. 'For a moment I felt like a hero!'

'But you were! You said you had a medal!'

'Yes. I had a medal, and I was proud of that, but I didn't feel like a hero. I felt a cheat, a fraud . . .'

'It's funny you should say that. That's what Mum used to say. I know it's different, because she was an actress and you were a soldier – but she was sort of famous – people used to point her out in the street and ask for her autograph and wave to her and she liked that, I know she did. But she often said, "I don't deserve this . . ." It made her nervous. She used to say, "I'm a cheat, really. I'm nothing special."'

'I can understand that,' he murmured.

'I can't! She wasn't a cheat . . . she never claimed to be a brilliant actress. She wanted to be one, maybe, but it was other people who said she was good. So how could she be a cheat? I mean, why weren't you a hero?'

'Why?' he laughed loudly, then said very coldly, 'How could any man do what I did and call himself a hero?'

'I don't understand.'

'You do.'

'But you got that medal – and you saved that man's life and you stayed with him till he died, didn't you?'

He watched me in silence.

'You're talking about . . . about the train, are you?' I said in the end. 'About getting on the train . . . and . . .'

'And?' His eyes never left my face.

'And . . . and not going back . . .'

'And?'

'And not helping them . . . your mother and brother. And . . .'

'Say it,' he said.

'And never ever seeing them again. Is that what happened?'

'Yes. That is exactly what happened.'

It was me who was crying, but I kept my head down, so maybe he didn't see me.

'Is that why you didn't feel like a hero?' I managed to ask finally.

'Of course.'

'But that's not fair, Mr Wassilewska. I mean, maybe you should have gone back – but you couldn't have known what was going to happen, could you? No one should be blamed for ever, just for making a mistake.'

'Shouldn't they?' he asked.

'No! No they shouldn't! No one should!'

We sat in silence for a long time and I thought about this as I turned the little bear round and round in my hand.

'Would you like to keep it?' he asked.

'No. No. It's yours,' I replied, quickly handing it back to him. 'You need him.'

'Do I?' he said, looking at it.

'Well,' I began carefully, 'in that case, if you don't really need him. I think I know who'd like him very much. My little brother would. He collects little animals like that. Mum sometimes used to bring them back for him.'

'All right then,' said Mr Wassilewska. 'That's a good idea, but you tell him from me that he must take good care of Voytek. He's very special.'

Later that night, I silently put the little bear on Benjy's pillow, as a surprise. When I crept back to my own bed I lay there and looked up at the stars and I wondered if she was somewhere out there, and could do that too.

13

Into the Cage

S HE WAS BACK. AS SUDDENLY AS SHE HAD GONE SHE HAD now returned. At first I didn't believe it. I rolled over and buried my face in my pillow and tried to sleep on. I'd dreamt of this before. I'd woken in the night, disturbed by her insistent voice. I'd caught my breath in the street because I'd seen her in the distance: that dark hair falling down on to those shoulders could only be hers, couldn't it? She'd held her head just like that. I'd even smelt her perfume on the bus. I turned round quickly, but I wasn't quick enough. I hadn't been able to see her, and the woman sitting behind me had met my stare with confident indifference.

'She's back!' Benjy was whispering hotly in my ear. He shook me again.

When I opened one eye, his little pink face was an inch from mine. I could feel his breath on my cheek.

'About time,' I said casually, but I didn't feel at all casual. It would serve her right if none of us even bothered to rush down and say hello.

I couldn't have believed that I could have felt so furious and so cruel or that Benjy could have looked so delighted.

'I'll be down soon,' I said. 'Why don't you go and pester her instead?' But when I opened my eyes again, he was still there, bending very close and watching me.

'Well, go on!' I muttered irritably. I certainly wasn't going to do the big reconciliation scene in my boxer shorts.

'She isn't here *now*,' said Benjy, patiently.

'What do you mean?'

'Well, she isn't *still* here. She had to go again.'

I began to swear, then I saw his face and stopped.

'Honestly,' he said in a very small voice, 'she isn't here any more. I've been down already and looked.'

Outside it was still dark.

'Did she leave something special for you as well?' he asked.

I shook my head.

'Never mind,' he said kindly. 'I expect she will.' He opened his hand and, of course, there it was: the little brown bear.

'That wasn't Mum,' I cried, but he wouldn't listen.

'It was! Honestly it was! She remembered that I like these little animal things. And she must have bought this one specially for me.'

'It's not even new,' I said. 'Look, it's chipped.'

His lip trembled for a moment.

'That's only because,' he said slowly, 'she's had to carry it around for ages waiting to come. I expect she just popped in and put it on my pillow and then had to go . . .'

It went on and on. I couldn't stop him. In the end I made up some story about the little bear being tired out and needing to hibernate, and he listened and yawned. We wrapped the tiny bear in a handkerchief and nestled it into the blue bed and then I persuaded Benjy to climb in beside it. In the morning, I promised, when it was light, I'd help him look again.

In the end he fell asleep with the bear firmly clasped in his hand. I half thought of taking it away in the night and trying to persuade him that he had imagined it all in some dream, but I didn't. Instead, when he was sound asleep and breathing evenly, I crept downstairs and looked into all the rooms, just in case.

I dreaded the morning, when Benjy would rush in and babble on about Mum, but it didn't happen like that. He brought the little bear down to breakfast and sat him on the edge of his cereal bowl and fed him drops of milk. When Tess asked him where he'd got it, he said that he'd found it in his bed. Auntie B remarked that it looked quite old and when she handed it on to me to inspect, I just said that it reminded me of something. Benjy grinned at me, as though we both shared some enormous secret. Then he dried the little bear on the edge of the tablecloth and put it safely away in his pocket.

Dad remarked that he was pleased that he hadn't been woken in the night by a bear in his half of the bed. Benjy giggled and I was glad to escape to Mr Wassilewska's.

The washing-up was still in the sink, so I thought I ought to offer to help. I was surprised that he accepted, and then there I was, stuck at the sink wearing a pair of yellow rubber gloves, with bubbles everywhere.

'I can see you're quite new to this.' He eyed me critically.

'I used to help Mum,' I said, 'sometimes. About Voytek,' I continued hurriedly. 'What happened to him after you left Glasgow?'

'After the march through the streets and the cheering crowds, you mean? First, of course, we all are put in an army camp and Voytek is with us. It's 1945 but the war is not over: fighting continues in Europe and the Far East but at least most people here are now daring to hope that the end is near. For Voytek, this is an easy time. He has settled in quite happily. For me, although I'm unlikely to fight again, it is a very difficult time.

The Scottish people are kind and welcoming, but it is still so hard. Each day brings us more news of terrible things happening in Poland. Soon we hear that the great cities of Poland, Warsaw, Lublin, even my town Lvov, have risen up against the Germans and have been destroyed and lost. Our worst fears are coming true. It will be too dangerous for us to go back. We hear that the Russian Army in Poland has arrested and taken away even the resistance fighters who have been fighting the Germans. We are unable to help and feel quite desperate.

Whenever I can, I drive out into the countryside. I climb the hillside covered first with heather and gorse, then, in the winter, whitened with frost and snow. I listen to this strange, impossible language, English. I eat this odd, tasteless food. I find that I am living among people who do not even know about pickled mushrooms and poppyseed cake. And little by little I accept that I must call all this, which is so different, "home".

Out on those hills, I write again and beg my fiancée to change her mind, to stay here with me, but she says she cannot do that. I find it very hard to accept. She and her brother do return to Poland. We correspond, but less and less over the months and years. She writes, eventually, that it makes problems for her to receive letters from abroad. I understand. Soon we are only sending a postcard at Christmas and at Easter. Then, even these do not come.

But I'm getting too far ahead. You asked me about Voytek. Poor Voytek! While we are worrying that we can never return home, because those homes have gone, we are also worrying about Voytek's future. The war in Europe finally ended in May 1945, and then we too must leave the army. We and thousands and thousands of others become civilians again. And so must Voytek. We soldiers cannot look after him any longer. It is clear that we must find a new home for him here. He can no more return to his home in the mountain caves of Persia, than I can return to mine in Poland. It is decided, eventually, that he must go to a zoo!'

'A zoo!' I was horrified. I didn't like zoos.

I had visited one with my class in primary school. I'd been so excited beforehand. I had imagined that the zoo would be full of really wild and extraordinary animals, such as we always saw on the television, and it wasn't. It was full of shrieking parrots, barking dogs, monkeys with enormous blue-and-red bottoms and this old, yellowed polar bear who sprawled on a pink, concrete rock and tossed its head about like a maniac. It had been a rotten place and it stank. We had spent all our time avoiding the animals and our teachers and escaping into the café for crisps and drinks. I remembered that we'd had most fun feeding crisps to the squabbling sparrows. The zoo animals had stared at us with boredom and dislike.

'A zoo!' I said again. 'How awful!'

Mr Wassilewska nodded.

'That is exactly what I thought: that it would be like prison for him. I was very upset. This animal has been with us for over three years. We have brought him up, and have hardly been apart. We've shared everything with him: our food and drink, our tents and our water. We've even shared the danger and sorrows of battle and the pleasures of peace. How, then, can this animal, who has been so free, be kept behind bars in a zoo? Even in a good zoo, like Edinburgh, it is a cruel prospect. It feels like a betrayal. And I cannot bear to do it.'

'Couldn't you have done something else?' I asked.

'We would, if we could have thought of it. But what do you suggest? We could not think of anything better.'

I couldn't either, but that didn't stop me from remembering the polar bear, endlessly, hopelessly, swinging its head to and fro.

'I bet Voytek was angry when you put him in the cage,' I said. 'I would have been furious!'

'That is what everybody expected. At the zoo, the keepers have ready the chains and the iron prods that they must sometimes use to get unwilling animals into a cage. It is a bleak November day, and they have been waiting for us to arrive, stamping their feet in the cold. They are pleased and proud to have been entrusted with Voytek, but they are a little anxious. Bears, they know, are never really tame: they're solitary creatures and are often dangerous. Now, they watch in amazement. Voytek jumps down from the lorry, looking very cheerful and energetic. It has been, after all, a great ride, right across Scotland, and he has always loved to travel with friends.

I remember to this day how he looked around him curiously, wrinkling his nose. There are lots of strange animal smells, lots of fascinating noises. In front of us is a dark, barred cage and beside it, with a curved wall running round, is his enclosure. There are some rocks in it, some tree-stumps and a concrete pool. I can hardly bring myself to watch. One of us walks into the cage and Voytek follows cheerfully, nibbling the tit bits we have brought with us. The zoo keepers stare: never have they seen an animal such as this walk so willingly into a cage. They are upset, but not as sad as we are. We stay on, fooling around with Voytek, wrestling with him one last time, trying at all costs to avoid the moment when we must leave him. But this moment comes too, in the end. One by one we slip out so quietly that he is not aware of it. When we turn to look back, he is sitting there, patiently, waiting for us to return. He doesn't protest. He looks around his enclosure and then back at us, and wants to know when he will be free.'

'And didn't that ever happen?'

'No. He was never free again. Of course in the zoo they were good to him – and he was a very popular animal. Lots of visitors liked to see him: I think they made these little china models of him because he was so popular and famous. Everybody loved that bear. Naturally, the Polish soldiers came to see him all the time – and drove the keepers crazy because they would climb over the barriers and wrestle and play with Voytek, just as they always had done. But it was not the same. Voytek was not free. It made us all very sad, and I hated it so much that for some time I stopped going to visit him.'

'What happened to him? Did he get ill or something?'

'No. That was what was so remarkable about that animal. You know, he couldn't have been really happy there, but he never became angry and mean. It was as though he understood that this was the best that could be done for him and he did not blame us.

Later, when I had time off, I would go secretly on my own and visit him. I missed him a great deal: I had told him things that I had not told to anyone else and although I could not do that now, I still found him a great comfort. I would look at him, in his cage, in this small stone world that gave him the smells and sounds of freedom, but not the feel of it, and I would tell myself that if this animal could begin a new life, with dignity and courage, then I could too. He gave me some of his courage. Maybe I am just a foolish old man, but that is what I really believe.'

'I don't think it's foolish,' I said. 'And I think it's still happening, in a way.'

Then I told him about Benjy and the little china bear and what had happened in the night.

'Last night Benjy seemed to think that Mum had come home,' I said, 'but this morning, he was different. It was as if he understood.'

I dried up the last cup and hung it on its hook.

'I really like it here,' I said, looking around. 'It feels different.'

'Oh dear,' he laughed, 'to think I've spent a lifetime trying to make it feel the same . . .'

'The same as what?'

'The same as our house in Lvov. The same as the home I left behind. I used to think about that house all the time. It began in Kazakhstan, as I told you. It was a way to pass the time. Later, in the desert and even during the unending bombardments of Monte Cassino, I rebuilt that house in my mind. I imagined every plank of wood and every tile, each cushion and even the shape of flowers sewn on them by my mother's hand. I remembered it all: the curved hinges on the shutters, the iron railing on the steps. I found them in my mind, as one finds forgotten letters at the back of a drawer. It was treasure, stored up.

Later, when I left the army in 1946, I worked as a miner in the north of England. Then, since I always wanted to build things, I joined another Pole and we started a small building business and it goes quite well: after years of war people need their houses repaired. We travelled around building, he and I. We are both restless, always talking of the day when we will return but never returning. Then my friend meets an English girl, they fall in love, they marry and he does not want to travel any more. He stays in the north. He buys a little house and works locally. I too have bought a little shabby house, but I cannot settle. I repair the house nicely, I sell it and I'm surprised: I have done well. I have made money. I try again and I make more money. Then I buy a big old house and I convert it into flats, and lots of people want to buy them. I sell one to Peter, my old friend – he too is married. Everybody is marrying, settling down with their families. Everybody except me. I am still moving on. My eyes are still on the horizon, still I'm scanning the crowds in the street, just in case. I'm hoping when there is no hope. Twenty years later, I'm still looking for a young woman whose dark hair is streaked with white and for a curly-haired small boy who will be running and laughing by her side.

And all through these years my old friend Voytek lives his quiet life in the zoo in Edinburgh. It is not so bad: he can watch the penguins near by and since his enclosure is on a bend in the path, a lot of people notice him and talk to him. He is very fond of children and many school classes come to see him, especially the children from the Polish schools: whenever he hears Polish spoken, he gets excited. When I am near Edinburgh, I always go and have a chat. One day, I tell him that I have seen this nice piece of land with a view down a valley. It is a large plot, still left empty after the war, and I'm thinking of buying it and building a house on it. He agrees with me and so this is what I do. Little by little, I build this house: the house that I have already in my head. For of course, if my family were to come, they would need a home, wouldn't they?'

'Is this house exactly the same as the new house your father built?'

'No. For one thing, how can we ever know if we have remembered anything exactly? I have no pictures and no photographs from that time. Peter was the only person who could remember my house and even he was never sure. But over the years it was built, though some parts, certainly, are quite different.'

'Like the steps!' I interrupted.

'Indeed. Those, I remembered from our old house in the town centre. I added them later because I needed a place where I could sit looking into the distance, and imagine myself back in that family group.'

'Dad always said that the steps had been added later.'

'Did he?'

I nodded, glad that I hadn't repeated Dad's opinion that the steps were 'pretentious'.

'But where did that photo of your old house come from, Mr Wassilewska? The photo of you as a little boy, with all your family? Did you go back after the war and get it?'

'No. Many times I planned to make a visit and I know

people who have done that. Peter and his wife went, but I have not.' He sighed. 'Maybe they are braver than I . . .'

'Or just different,' I suggested.

'Maybe. Anyway, I never revisited my home, or only in my dreams. I shall never walk along that road again. The photo which you speak of was in my grandmother's house and she gave it to my sister . . .'

'To Stanislawa?'

'No, to Maria. To my little sister.'

In the silence I, too, saw a small girl in a rabbit-skin cap, reaching out beyond the silence of the crowd.

'No, it was not Stanislawa. Stanislawa, who always laughed, did not come back. Of we six children only two survived the war. You know that Edward, who was in Siberia, died of his wounds on the slopes of Monte Cassino. Jan, I learnt later, had joined the underground resistance fighters, and died in Warsaw in 1944, in the uprising. Stanislawa was arrested. She and maybe her baby died in the camps. Only Maria and I survived the war, and she was never in good health. She stayed on the farm with our grandmother after the war and times were hard for both of them. She suffered badly from her nerves and was never so strong after she had been in prison as a tiny child. We write, at Christmas. She sent that photograph to me. She even came, once, to visit me here, but it was too difficult: too much to say and both of us, perhaps, finding a stranger where we had longed to find a friend. And she has her own family.'

'And . . . ? I began but couldn't continue.

'And Josef?' he suggested, 'and what happened to Josef and my mother?'

I nodded, unable to speak.

'I don't know. Not for sure. Not finally. I know of no grave, no name on any list, no one who remembers their last days. It is almost certain that they died of illness and exhaustion in that town in Uzbekistan, on the way to freedom. With winter coming on, it would have been so very hard for them, and thousands and thousands of Poles died on those journeys. They died within sight of help – just as we see people die today.

'After the war ended, there were so many, many people all over the world, who never knew for sure what had happened to their families and their friends. And many, like me, must always think that if only they had done this, or that, then, it might all have been different.'

'Do you still think that, Mr Wassilewska?'

'Yes. If I am honest. It does not hurt as much, and it does not hurt all the time. But since you ask me, yes! I still feel guilty. It is something that I try never to speak of, or even to think of. It makes me unwell.

'Probably, it is that which has made me a little ill after my visit to Peter and his wife. It is like an old wound: the scar on the surface has almost faded, but sometimes it catches you out when you least expect it. In the pleasure of seeing them, the pain awakes. I shall always regret that I did not go back to help them.'

'Do you think that Mum will feel like that?' Suddenly, as I spoke, I realized that the thought gave me no pleasure at all.

'Because,' I continued, 'I think she went away before. I don't know when, and Dad never talks about it, but I'm sure I'm right. And why did she ask you about being homesick?'

I didn't give him time to reply; already some of the answers were becoming clearer.

'She must have known that she was going to leave us, mustn't she? She was already thinking about it and she was afraid of being homesick –'

It was like finding her, almost, in the darkened room. It was like feeling her near me again.

'Please tell me, Mr Wassilewska.'

He still didn't answer.

'That night, years ago, when Mum was in the garden with Tess and I was asleep in bed, what happened when you spoke to her?'

He remained silent, forcing me to feel my way forward, inch by inch.

'You heard crying and you looked over the fence, didn't you, and thought for a moment that you were seeing somebody else. You mistook Mum for your fiancée, for the dark-haired girl who went back to Poland. So you stared and asked her who she was and then you asked if she wanted to live in your house. You wanted Mum, and us, to come and live happily in this house which you'd been getting ready for a family who could never come. Only Mum didn't understand that. She got upset and ran indoors and Dad came round to you later, and you explained that you only wanted to sell the house to us –'

We had left the kitchen with its warm wooden carvings and its tiles of unfading flowers and we were in the empty centre of the house with its few old pictures clinging coldly to the plain walls.

'I was not interested in money or anything like that,' he said. 'I just thought that it would be nice for this house to have children running through it. I had built a castle of dreams that I couldn't complete. Look around you: I have given up. I made part of the house perfect, but I couldn't go on. Perhaps I was just foolish.'

We were standing out on the step.

'Mum hated the idea, I mean, we weren't allowed to set foot in here. She'd be wild if she knew I was here now. Why was that? Why did she feel like that, Mr Wassilewska?'

'She came to see me –'

'I didn't know.'

'Why should you? You were still a baby. She came back to see me the next day. She questioned me and I told

—— 153 ——

her a little about myself – that I was still restless, that still I must sit on the step and watch the horizon. I think that maybe she recognised herself in me – and I think she was afraid of what she saw. She was afraid that I understood her. Maybe we do not like people to understand all our secrets.'

'And her secret,' I said, 'was her unhappiness, and you'd understood that. She'd always wanted to go away, hadn't she? Even then, when I was really small . . .' It was so sad that I didn't want to think about it.

Down by the pond something was moving amongst the reeds. Mr Wassilewska pointed and I was glad to be distracted.

'I think,' he said, 'that it is the goldfish thief again. Perhaps you can tell him that they've had enough excitement for the moment?'

'All right. But do you mind if I come tomorrow, to hear what happened in the end? Especially to Voytek.'

'No, I don't mind at all. And maybe you should invite the thief?'

'What? Here?' I was outraged, at first.

'Why not? He might like to hear something about a bear.'

'Oh, I don't think so,' I said quickly.

'You know best.' He turned to go in.

'I suppose,' I called back, 'you could tell him a sort of child's version –'

'Or you could,' he said softly.

I was going to protest but I didn't. I thought about what he'd said as I walked down to the reeds where Benjy was grinning up at me.

14

A View of Stars

'YOU NEVER GUESSED THAT I WAS HIDING IN THERE, did you?' asked Benjy proudly. He caught up with me as I was trying to squeeze back through the fence. It had come on to rain in great, windy gusts. He sniffed noisily.

'When I'm grown up,' he said, 'that's what I'm going to do.'

'What?'

'Track people. I'm going to follow them. I'll be a sort of detective and follow clues and footprints and find people. And animals, if it's in the jungle. Because I'm good at hiding. And . . .'

'Shut up,' I gasped. I'd got stuck halfway and the drips were running off the fence and down the back of my neck.

I forced my shoulders through, but as I shifted my weight to try and get one leg clear, something caught, ripped and then held firm. When I tried to wriggle clear the whole fence creaked ominously.

'And I'll get rewards, won't I? Won't I? Richard, you do get rewards for finding people's purses and treasures and lost dogs, don't you? Richard?'

'Do shut up, Benjy,' I said, 'I'm stuck.'

He was watching me with cheerful interest. The rain

ran off his soaked hair and on to his sodden anorak. His nose was bright red. He sniffed again and licked a drip from the tip. I wondered how long he'd been out there, hiding in the reeds. His fingers were puffy with cold. I hoped that Auntie B wouldn't blame me.

'You're too big to be doing that,' he remarked.

He was, I reflected grimly, quite right.

'Do you think,' I said, 'you could just give me a shove? Please?'

His face lit up. 'Me? Really? Are you sure?' he chewed his lip, sizing up the prospect.

'Sure I'm sure. But just a little one.'

He took a large step back in his red wellingtons. Then he stamped out a patch amongst the fallen leaves with all the gravity of a striker taking a free kick at a cup final. He made that revving-up noise which little kids do. Then he charged with his head down, but stopped at the last moment and squatted beside me.

'You're not stuck,' he observed, 'you're caught.'

'Caught? Where?'

'It's your belt, I think. It's caught on this bit of wood.'

'Can't you fix it?' I couldn't even turn round to investigate.

'Me?' he asked. 'Do you want *me* to fix it?'

'Why not? I don't see anybody else mad enough to be out in this rain,' I muttered. 'Anyway, it's good practice for being a detective.'

'Is it?' He knelt down in the mud and set to work enthusiastically.

The wind and rain had brought down the rest of the apples. I could smell their sharp juices as they lay split and bruised beneath the trees. Next week we'd all be back at school. I'd been thinking about cycling there this term. I decided that I wouldn't ask Dad for permission. I'd just announce that that was what I was going to do. After all, school lets us, if we wear helmets. And why shouldn't I? I was sick to death of waiting for the bus.

'I've done it!' Benjy shrieked, and he had.

I stood up and stretched gratefully. I was just wondering if the tyres on my bike were all right when for no reason at all Benjy burst into tears. I thought he must have run a splinter into his finger, but he was crying so much that I couldn't understand a word that he said. He'd run back to the fence and scrambled through and was digging about desperately amongst the wet leaves and the worm-casts.

'It's my bear,' he sobbed. 'I've lost my special bear.'

We searched until it was pitch dark but we didn't find it. He was inconsolable. It upset me. I wanted him to stop crying. I'd have said anything.

'Look,' I began, 'I'm sure that Mum will, well, will bring another. Or one like it. When she comes next time . . .'

He rubbed his sleeve over his swollen face and stopped crying, though his breath still came in painful, dry sobs.

'I'm sure you can find other little bears just like that one. Or nicer.'

I was already planning a speedy trip to the High Street. I didn't care what it cost. I only wanted him to stop crying.

'We could go and look together,' I said.

He didn't reply but looked up towards the house. Auntie B and Dad were moving about in the lighted kitchen, getting supper. From an upstairs window, maybe in Tess's room, music floated. My feet felt really wet.

'Come on, Benjy,' I said giving him a gentle tug. 'I'm sure we can find another.'

'She didn't *really* bring it, did she?' He pulled away from me.

'Well –' I didn't know what to say.

'And she didn't send me a card. Even for my special

birthday. It was special, wasn't it, Richard? That eight, eight, eight-eight is special, isn't it?'

'Yes. It's very special.'

'Then why didn't she?'

'I don't know. But I'm sure she wanted to.'

He reached out in the dark and found my arm and clung so close that I'm sure he was wiping his nose on my sleeve.

'Do you think she's . . .' he breathed the words so quietly that they almost hadn't been spoken.

'No,' I said clearly. 'No. I know she isn't. I'm sure of it. But she *has* gone away.'

'Where?'

'I don't know. But I'm sure she thinks about us.'

'I don't think about *her*,' he said fiercely, 'ever.'

'I do,' I whispered. 'I think about her all the time. And in the night, when I wake up and miss her, I look out at the stars and I remember that wherever she is, she can look out and see them too.'

He tilted his head right back and swallowed and gazed up. Then Tess opened the back door and called out that supper was ready and would we please hurry up. I pulled him gently and this time we went in together.

I couldn't go round to Mr Wassilewska's for several days after that. Benjy developed a rotten cold and since it was partly my fault I felt that I should stay around and try to keep him occupied. The doctor said that he was a typical 'tonsillitis tyrant': being sick one moment and demanding food that he couldn't swallow the next. Then Tess and Dad sickened and took to their beds. Poor Auntie B was so worn out that one morning I noticed that she'd actually fallen asleep, sitting upright at the breakfast table. I felt quite sorry for her and did a whole load of washing-up. The rest of the time I spent dishing out tissues and taking away scummy cups of tea.

Then, one evening, Benjy turned up at my bedroom

door. He had a pleading look on his face and Mum's special pillow clasped to his chest. He wanted to move back in. I wasn't keen, but I had to admit that Dad was very pathetic when he was ill. I couldn't blame Benjy for decamping. Dad's cough reminded me of a car that's lost its silencer.

'But you'll have to shut up,' I said, 'when I'm busy.'

'I promise. And I'm good at shutting up, aren't I? Aren't I, Richard? When you say "shut up", I'll shut up. So go on.'

'Go on what?'

'Say "shut up", and I will, honestly. But I've got to be talking first, haven't I? If I'm not talking, I can't shut up. Can I? Can I, Richard?'

'Shut up!'

He did stop. I have to admit that as well, though he started again two seconds later. Still, I was glad that at least he looked a bit better.

That night I heard the phone ring again. I opened my eyes in sudden terror as the sound dragged me from the safe warmth of sleep. This time I'd let someone else get up, but they didn't. I imagined her in some other room, in some distant place. I saw her hand slowly dial our number. Her dark head would be inclined to one side as she listened to the unanswered ring. Then, at the exact moment when I awoke, she would sigh and replace the receiver and walk away.

If it hadn't all been a dream.

'Benjy? Did you hear that?' He didn't stir.

I went downstairs and turned on the hall light. I dialled the recall number which tells you the number of the last call made to that phone. And it wasn't from her. I couldn't think why I hadn't done this before. The last call to our phone was from the Edwardses, four doors away. I even remembered it, because Auntie B and I had laughed about it: Mrs Edwards had wanted to know if, perhaps, by any remote chance, she'd left one of her cake plates with us. I'd promised to have a look. And nobody had called us after that.

I was glad. Instead of being disappointed, it felt as if a great weight had been lifted from me. She wasn't silently calling us in the desperate loneliness of the night in a way that must always remain unanswered.

It was cold downstairs and I shivered and nipped back up.

'Benjy?'

But he wasn't in the little blue bed. The moonlight streamed in through the open curtains and I felt the dent in the pillow where his head had been. It was cold.

'Benjy?'

I peeped into Dad's room first and then all the others. Had he got worse and gone delirious? Was he sleep-walking? Or . . . ?

I ran frantically back down the stairs. I was already saying 'No' to myself. No, she couldn't have done that. She wouldn't have come in the night and taken him away too. That was the madness of dreams and I wasn't going to believe them any longer.

The back door was wide open. I ran out into the chill dawn and followed his tracks to the bottom of the garden. I squeezed through the fence and ran on over Mr Wassilewska's dew-soaked lawn. The tracks led towards the pond. There, through the reeds which grew thickly at the edge, I could see something pale lying in the water.

My fear was so intense that I've no recollection of how I went towards the reeds. I was drawn over the ice-cold, shimmering grass, step by step, as though someone unseen were reeling me in, hand over hand.

It was her pillow. It was her special, silky pillow, floating on the quiet surface of the pond. Underneath the fish nibbled the trailing ribbons and the lace with round, astonished eyes.

He was curled up in the deck-chair on the top of the steps. One foot stuck out from beneath the old camel-hair rug. I wanted to thump him. Instead, I shouted.

'I don't see why you're making such a fuss,' he yawned. 'You sit on his chairs all the time. And you borrow his rug. I've seen you, Richard. I've seen you from the top of the apple tree. So why can't I?'

'Because it's the middle of the night!' I yelled.

'It isn't.'

'Anyway,' I said, glancing at my watch, 'you left the back door open. And you've been ill. You could get pneumonia.'

'But I found it.'

'Found what?'

'My little Voytek, of course. I knew I would. I told you I'd be a good detective. You didn't believe me, but I found it. Look!'

He opened his muddy hand and there it was: the little chipped model of the bear, with a trail of pondweed still wrapped around it.

'I'm so glad,' I said.

'You won't tell them, will you?' he begged as we went back down the garden.

'I should.'

'But they'll be furious. Especially Dad.'

'Why?'

'Because it was her *special* pillow,' he mumbled.

I had to laugh then.

'I didn't mean to, honestly, Richard. It just fell in, all by itself, when I was leaning over to get my bear out. Because I remembered in the night. I woke up and I was thinking about that star thing and then I suddenly remembered that I hadn't put him back in my pocket. I'd put him in the pond to have a look at the goldfish, because they'd be like whales to him, wouldn't they? And I forgot him. Then I remembered. I remembered exactly

—— 161 ——

where he was, on the rock and I had to go and get him because he'd been out there all night. I had to get him, didn't I, Richard?'

I squeezed the pillow out wearily, then hid it up in the apple tree, out of sight, and I promised not to say a word.

The invalids had been restored to health and we'd been back at school for a couple of days before I managed to get over to Mr Wassilewska. The start of term is always busy and it seemed as if we would have more homework than last year. And I was cycling. But it wasn't just that. Something else had happened. A new girl called Maya had come into our class. She told me that she hadn't been in England long. And she cycled. And even if she hadn't been passing our house every day I'd still have wanted to be friendly. I know lots of people don't believe in love at first sight, but I think that maybe I do. Anyway, it didn't leave me much time.

On Saturday, I was feeling so guilty about Mr Wassilewska that I got up extra early. I'd have time to visit him before I met Maya. I'd promised to show her a quieter route into school. Everybody else was asleep. I'd made a cup of tea and was eating breakfast cereal straight from the packet. I'd just crammed an enormous handful into my mouth when I heard the post falling on to the mat.

The blue edge of a postcard lay amongst the usual heap of bills and advertisements for things that we would never want. It was a colour photograph of a velvet night above a small mountain village. The little white houses clustered and clung to the steep, rocky sides as though they sought shelter before a coming storm. She'd printed our address and our names in her neat, clear hand. She had sent 'love and best wishes' and had remembered to wish us a 'happy autumn term'. The stamp was Italian and it had been franked in Rome but I knew at once what it portrayed. I'd already seen the abbey on the top of the mountain. I could have torn it up. I could have ripped it into tiny pieces and dropped them one by one into the gutter outside the house, but I didn't. I read it again and again. When I knew every word by heart I looked at the picture and thought of all the things that her card did not say.

Upstairs a door opened. I quickly propped the postcard against the milk bottle and fled. I couldn't bear any more, not then.

When Mr Wassilewska opened his door I started speaking at once. I apologised for staying away; I made excuses, telling him how busy I'd been. 'But I do want to hear the end of the story,' I said.

'I thought you knew it,' he replied.

I was hurt. I was afraid that he was tired of talking to me and that he wanted to be left alone.

'It isn't for me. It's for Benjy. He needs to know.'

'In that case, I'll try again.'

He opened up the two chairs but he didn't begin.

'You'd got to the cage,' I prompted him. 'Voytek had gone into his cage and you'd built this house . . .'

He remained silent.

'You used to go up to visit Voytek. Your sister, Maria, visited you here in England, but you didn't return to Poland. Did you?'

He only shook his head.

'And you were working on this house. Peter had got married, but you were still working on this house, and . . .'

He wouldn't speak. I felt very uncomfortable. It was like struggling against a strong wind, when no hand is held out to help.

'You'd stopped writing to that girl, and Voytek was still in the cage and . . .'

'And I too.'

'You?' I didn't want to understand him. Hurriedly, I

—— 163 ——

asked more questions about Voytek and this time he answered.

'That bear lived in the zoo for over twenty years, I believe. At the end of his life he was quite sick and no longer came out to entertain his public. When he was too ill, he was put down, shot, I believe. And I don't suppose that it would have been much different if he had remained in Persia. I think that the hunters would have got him in the end there too.

'But while he was alive he lived with such great courage and I admired him so much for that. Sometimes I think that he lived with more courage than me. Certainly, he adapted to his new home in a new land: a new chance in another land. That was what the guard said to us, when we first arrived in Kazakhstan. Do you remember?'

I nodded.

'I tried to adapt,' he said, 'but when I think about it now, it seems that it is I who remained in the cage. I built memories and dreams into bars which held me back from the present. And maybe, for me, that was the way it had to be, but I would be sad if I thought that anyone else, especially anyone young, was going to follow my path too closely.'

'Is that what I should . . . tell Benjy?'

'Why not? We must never forget the past, but we must try to leave it in its own quiet place. When we drag it with us, the burden is sometimes too heavy.'

'Do you think that Benjy could understand that if I told him?'

'Josef did.'

For a moment I, too, thought I heard them calling, thought I saw them reaching out from the silence of the crowd.

We sat side by side in the slanting sun. Mist lay in the valley and I could smell autumn. When I looked at Mr

Wassilewska, his eyes were closed and he had pulled the rug around himself as if he felt cold.

'She sent a postcard,' I said at last. 'It came this morning.'

He waited for me.

'She sent love and best wishes and hoped we'd have a happy autumn term. But that was all. She's not coming back, is she, Mr Wassilewska? Not now.'

I thought that I had heard someone call my name, so I stood up. 'And do you know what? The card is from Monte Cassino. The picture shows the abbey and the little village at night. That's where you fought, wasn't it? And wasn't it destroyed? But it's been rebuilt. Don't you think it's strange that she should send that card to us?'

'Is it?' he asked. He wasn't surprised and then I understood that it wasn't strange either.

Then I heard someone calling my name: Benjy was running up the garden with the card in his hand. Mr Wassilewska looked at me but I knew what I was going to do. When Benjy stopped talking for two seconds I would point out that if he looked very carefully, there were tiny gold stars shining in the dark blue sky.